THE TOR DOUBLES

Tor is proud to bring you the best in science fiction's short novels. An amazing amount of particularly fine science fiction is written at a length just too short to put in a book by itself, so we're providing them two at a time.

The Tor Doubles will be both new stories and older ones, all carefully chosen. Whichever side you start with, you will be able to turn the book over and enjoy the other side just as much.

The Clock Was Counting Backward

A hundred seconds to entry. For better or worse, he was committed. In a minute and a half, he would graze the Jovian atmosphere and would be caught irrevocably in the grip of the giant.

The countdown was two seconds late—not at all bad, considering the unknowns involved. Beyond the walls of the capsule came a ghostly sighing that rose steadily to a high-pitched screaming roar. The noise was quite different from that of a re-entry on Earth or Mars; in this thin atmosphere of hydrogen and helium, all sounds were transformed a couple of octaves higher. On Jupiter, even thunder would have falsetto overtones.

ARTHUR C. CLARKE

A MEETING WITH MEDUSA

A TOM DOHERTY ASSOCIATES BOOK
NEW YORK

Reprinted by permission of the author's agent, Scott Meredith
Literary Agency.

A MEETING WITH MEDUSA

A TOR Book
Published by Tom Doherty Associates, Inc.
49 West 24 Street
New York, NY 10010

Cover art by Vincent di Fate

ISBN: 0-812-53362-3   Can. ISBN: 0-812-55967-3

Library of Congress Catalog Card Number: 88-50473

First edition: October 1988

Printed in the United States of America

0 9 8 7 6 5 4 3 2 1

A Day to Remember

THE *QUEEN ELIZABETH* WAS FIVE KILOMETERS ABOVE THE Grand Canyon, dawdling along at a comfortable 180, when Howard Falcon spotted the camera platform closing in from the right. He had been expecting it—nothing else was cleared to fly at this altitude—but he was not too happy to have company. Although he welcomed any signs of public interest, he also wanted as much empty sky as he could get. After all, he was the first man in history to navigate a ship half a kilometer long.

So far, this first test flight had gone perfectly; ironically enough, the only problem had been the century-old aircraft carrier *Chairman Mao,* borrowed from the San Diego naval museum for support operations. Only one of *Mao's* four nuclear reactors was still operating, and the old battlewagon's top speed was barely thirty knots. Luckily, wind speed at sea level had been less than half this, so it had not been too difficult to maintain still air on the flight deck. Though there had been a few anxious moments during gusts, when the mooring lines had been dropped, the great dirigible had risen smoothly, straight up into the sky, as if on an invisible elevator. If all went well, *Queen Elizabeth* IV would not meet *Chairman Mao* for another week.

Everything was under control: all test instruments gave normal readings. Commander Falcon decided to go upstairs and watch the rendezvous. He handed over to his second officer and walked out into the transparent tubeway that led through the heart of the ship. There, as always, he was overwhelmed by the spectacle of the largest space ever enclosed by man.

The ten spherical gas cells, each more than 100 meters across, were ranged one behind the other like a line of gigantic soap bubbles. The tough plastic was so clear that he could see through the whole length of the array and make out details of the elevator mechanism almost half a kilometer from his vantage point. All around him, like a three-dimensional maze, was the structural framework of the ship—the great longitudinal girders running from nose to tail, the fifteen hoops that were the ribs of this skyborne colossus, whose varying sizes defined its graceful, streamlined profile.

At this low speed, there was very little sound—merely the soft rush of wind over the envelope and an occasional creak of metal as the pattern of stresses changed. The shadowless light from the rows of lamps far overhead gave the whole scene a curiously submarine quality, and to Falcon this was enhanced by the spectacle of the translucent gasbags. He had once encountered a squadron of large but harmless jelly-fish, pulsing their mindless way above a shallow tropical reef, and the plastic bubbles that gave *Queen Elizabeth* her lift often reminded him of these—especially when changing pressures made them crin-kle and scatter new patterns of light.

He walked fifty meters down the axis of the ship, until he came to the forward elevator, between gas cells one and two. Riding up to the observation deck, he noticed that it was uncomfortably hot and dictated a brief memo to himself on his pocket recorder. The *Queen* obtained almost a quarter of her buoyancy from the unlimited amounts of waste heat produced by her fusion power plant; on this lightly loaded flight, indeed, only six of the ten gas cells contained helium and the remaining four were full of air; yet she still carried 200 tons of water as ballast. However, running the cells at high temperatures did produce problems in refrigerating the accessways; it was obvious that a little more work would have to be done here.

A refreshing blast of cooler air hit him in the face when he stepped out onto the observation deck and into the dazzling sunlight streaming through the Plex-iglas roof. Half a dozen workmen, with an equal number of superchimp assistants, were busily laying the partly completed dance floor, while others were installing electric wiring and fixing furniture. It was a scene of controlled chaos and Falcon found it hard to believe that everything would be ready for the maiden voyage, only four weeks ahead. Well, that was not *his* problem, thank goodness. He was merely the captain, not the cruise director.

The human workers waved to him and the simps flashed toothy smiles as he walked through the confusion into the already completed sky lounge. This was his favorite place in the whole ship and he knew that once she was operating, he would never again have it all to himself. He would allow himself just five minutes of private enjoyment.

He called the bridge, checked that everything was still in order and relaxed into one of the comfortable swivel chairs. Below, in a curve that delighted the eye, was the unbroken silver sweep of the ship's envelope. He was perched at the highest point, surveying the whole immensity of the largest vehicle ever built. And when he had tired of *that*—all the way out to the horizon was the fantastic wilderness carved by the Colorado River in half a billion years of time.

Apart from the camera platform (it had now fallen back and was filming from amidships), he had the sky to himself. It was blue and empty, clear down to the horizon. In his grandfather's day, Falcon knew, it would have been streaked with vapor trails and stained with smoke. Both had gone; the aerial garbage had vanished with the primitive technologies that spawned it, and the long-distance transportation of this age arced too far beyond the stratosphere for any sight or sound of it to reach Earth. Once again, the lower atmosphere belonged to the birds and the clouds—and now to *Queen Elizabeth* IV.

It was true, as the old pioneers had said at the beginning of the twentieth century; this was the only way to travel—in silence and luxury, breathing the air around you and not cut off from it, near enough to the surface to watch the ever-changing beauty of land and sea. The subsonic jets of the 1980s, packed with hundreds of passengers seated ten abreast, could not even begin to match such comfort and spaciousness.

Of course, the *Q. E.* would never be an economic proposition; and even if her projected sister ships were built, only a few of the world's quarter of a billion inhabitants would ever enjoy this silent gliding through the sky. But a secure and prosperous global society could afford such follies and, indeed, needed them for its novelty and entertainment. There were at least a million men on Earth whose discretionary income exceeded a thousand new dollars a year, so the *Queen* would not lack for passengers.

Falcon's pocket communicator beeped; the copilot was calling from the bridge.

"OK for rendezvous, Captain? We've got all the data we need from this run and the TV people are getting impatient."

Falcon glanced at the camera platform, now matching his speed a quarter of a kilometer away.

"OK," he replied. "Proceed as arranged. I'll watch from here."

He walked back through the busy chaos of the observation deck, so that he could have a better view amidships. As he did so, he could feel the change of vibration underfoot; by the time he had reached the rear of the lounge, the ship had come to rest. Using his master key, he let himself out onto the small external platform flaring from the end of the deck; half a dozen people could stand there, with only low guardrails separating them from the vast sweep of the envelope —and from the ground, thousands of meters below. It was an exciting place to be and perfectly safe even when the ship was traveling at speed, for it was in the dead air behind the huge dorsal blister of the observation deck. Nevertheless, it was not intended that the passengers would have access to it; the view was a little too vertiginous.

The covers of the forward cargo hatch had already opened like giant trap doors and the camera platform was hovering above them, preparing to descend. Along this route, in the years to come, would travel thousands of passengers and tons of supplies; only on rare occasions would the *Queen* drop down to sea level and dock with her floating base.

A sudden gust of crosswind slapped Falcon's cheek and he tightened his grip on the guardrail. The Grand Canyon was a bad place for turbulence, though he did not expect much at this altitude. Without any real anxiety, he focused his attention on the descending platform, now about fifty meters above the ship. He knew that the highly skilled operator who was flying the remotely controlled vehicle had performed this very simple maneuver a dozen times already; it was inconceivable that he would have any difficulties.

Yet he seemed to be reacting rather sluggishly; that last gust had drifted the platform almost to the edge of the open hatchway. Surely the pilot could have corrected before this . . . did he have a control problem? It was very unlikely; these remotes had multiple-redundancy, fail-safe take-overs and any number of backup systems. Accidents were almost unheard of.

But there he went again, off to the left. Could the pilot be *drunk?* Improbable though that seemed, Falcon considered it seriously for a moment. Then he reached for his microphone switch.

Once again, without warning, he was slapped violently in the face. He hardly felt it, for he was staring in horror at the camera platform. The distant operator was fighting for control, trying to balance the craft on its jets—but he was only making matters worse. The oscillations increased—twenty degrees, forty, sixty, ninety . . .

"Switch to automatic, you fool!" Falcon shouted uselessly into his microphone. "Your manual control's not working!"

The platform flipped over onto its back; the jets no longer supported it but drove it swiftly downward. They had suddenly become allies of the gravity they had fought until this moment.

Falcon never heard the crash, though he felt it; he was already inside the observation deck, racing for the elevator that would take him down to the bridge. Workmen shouted at him anxiously, asking what had happened. It would be many months before he knew the answer to that question.

Just as he was stepping into the elevator cage, he changed his mind. What if there were a power failure? Better be on the safe side, even if it took longer and time was of the essence. He began to run down the spiral stairway enclosing the shaft.

Halfway down, he paused for a second to inspect the damage. That damned platform had gone clear through the ship, rupturing two of the gas cells as it did so. They were still collapsing slowly, in great falling veils of plastic. He was not worried about the loss of lift—the ballast could easily take care of that, as long as eight cells remained intact. Far more serious was the possibility of structural damage; already he could hear the great latticework around him groaning and protesting under its abnormal loads. It was not enough to have sufficient lift; unless it was properly distributed, the ship would break her back.

He was just resuming his descent when a superchimp, shrieking with fright, came racing down the elevator shaft, moving with incredible speed hand over hand along the *outside* of the latticework. In its terror, the poor beast had torn off its company uniform, perhaps in an unconscious attempt to regain the freedom of its ancestors.

Falcon, still descending as swiftly as he could, watched its approach with some alarm; a distraught simp was a powerful and potentially dangerous animal, especially if fear overcame its conditioning. As it overtook him, it started to call out a string of words, but they were all jumbled together and the only one he could recognize was a plaintive, frequently repeated "Boss." Even now, Falcon realized, it looked toward humans for guidance; he felt sorry for the creature, involved in a man-made disaster beyond its comprehension and for which it bore no responsibility.

It stopped opposite him, on the other side of the lattice; there was nothing to prevent it from coming through the open framework if it wished. Now its face was only inches from his and he was looking straight into the terrified eyes. Never before had he been so close to a simp and able to study its features in such detail; he felt that strange mingling of kinship and discomfort that all men experience when they gaze thus into the mirror of time.

His presence seemed to have calmed the creature; Falcon pointed up the shaft, back toward the observation deck, and said very clearly and precisely: "Boss —boss—*go.*" To his relief, the simp understood; it gave him a grimace that might have been a smile and at once started to race back the way it had come. Falcon had given it the best advice he could; if any safety remained aboard the *Queen*, it was in that direction. But his duty lay in the other.

He had almost completed his descent when, with a sound of rending metal, the vessel pitched nose down and the lights went out. But he could still see quite well, for a shaft of sunlight streamed through the open hatch and the huge tear in the envelope. Many years ago, he had stood in a great cathedral nave, watching the light pouring through the stained-glass windows and forming pools of multicolored radiance on the ancient flagstones. The dazzling shaft of sunlight through the ruined fabric high above reminded him of that moment. He was in a cathedral of metal, falling down the sky.

When he reached the bridge and was able for the first time to look outside, he was horrified to see how close the ship was to the ground. Only a thousand meters below were the beautiful and deadly pinnacles of rock and the red rivers of mud that were still carving their way down into the past. There was no level area anywhere in sight where a ship as large as the *Queen* could come to rest on an even keel.

A glance at the display board told him that all the ballast had gone. However, rate of descent had been reduced to a few meters a second; they still had a fighting chance.

Without a word, Falcon eased himself into the pilot's seat and took over such control as remained. The instrument board showed him everything he wished to know; speech was superfluous. In the back-

ground, he could hear the communications officer
giving a running report over the radio. By this time,
all the news channels of Earth would have been
preempted and he could imagine the utter frustration
of the program controllers. One of the most spectacular wrecks in history was occurring—without a single
camera to record it. The last moments of the *Queen*
would never fill millions with awe and terror, as had
those of the *Hindenburg* a century and a half before.

Now the ground was only half a kilometer away,
still coming up slowly. Though he had full thrust, he
had not dared use it, lest the weakened structure
collapse; but now he realized that he had no choice.
The wind was taking them toward a fork in the
canyon, where the river was split by a wedge of rock,
like the prow of some gigantic, fossilized ship of stone.
If she continued on her present course, the *Queen*
would straddle that triangular plateau and come to
rest with at least a third of her length jutting out over
nothingness; she would snap like a rotten stick.

From far away, above the sound of straining metal
and escaping gas, came the familiar whistle of the jets
as Falcon opened up the lateral thrusters. The ship
staggered and began to slew to port. The shriek of
tearing metal was now almost continuous—and the
rate of descent had started to increase ominously. A
glance at the damage-control board showed that cell
number five had just gone.

The ground was only meters away; even now, he
could not tell whether his maneuver would succeed or
fail. He switched the thrust vectors over to vertical,
giving maximum lift to reduce the force of impact.

The crash seemed to last forever. It was not violent

—merely prolonged and irresistible. It seemed that the whole universe was falling about them.

The sound of crunching metal came nearer, as if some great beast were eating its way through the dying ship.

Then floor and ceiling closed upon him like a vise.

"Because It's There"

"WHY DO YOU WANT TO GO TO JUPITER?"

"As Springer said when he lifted for Pluto—
because it's there."

"Thanks. Now we've got *that* out of the way—the
real reason." Howard Falcon smiled, though only
those who knew him well could have interpreted the
slight, leathery grimace. Webster was one of them; for
more than twenty years, they had been involved in
each other's projects. They had shared triumphs and
disasters—including the greatest disaster of all.

"Well, Springer's cliché is still valid. We've landed
on all the terrestrial planets but none of the gas giants.
They are the only real challenge left in the Solar
System."

"An expensive one. Have you worked out the cost?"

"As well as I can; here are the estimates. But
remember—this isn't a one-shot mission but a trans-

portation system. Once it's proved out, it can be used over and over again. And it will open up not merely Jupiter but *all* the giants."

Webster looked at the figures and whistled.

"Why not start with an easier planet—Uranus, for example? Half the gravity and less than half the escape velocity. Quieter weather, too—if that's the right word for it."

Webster had certainly done his homework. But that, of course, was why he was head of Long Range Planning.

"There's very little saving, when you allow for the extra distance and the logistics problems. For Jupiter, we can use the facilities on Ganymede. Beyond Saturn, we'd have to establish a new supply base."

Logical, thought Webster; but he was sure that it was not the important reason. Jupiter was lord of the Solar System; Falcon would be interested in no lesser challenge.

"Besides," Falcon continued, "Jupiter is a major scientific scandal. It's more than a hundred years since its radio storms were discovered, but we still don't know what causes them—and the Great Red Spot is as big a mystery as ever. That's why I can get matching funds from the Bureau of Astronautics. Do you know how many probes they have dropped into that atmosphere?"

"A couple of hundred, I believe."

"*Three* hundred and twenty-six, over the past fifty years—about a quarter of them total failures. Of course, they've learned a hell of a lot, but they've barely scratched the planet. Do you realize how *big* it is?"

"More than ten times the size of Earth."

"Yes, yes—but do you know what that really means?"

Falcon pointed to the large globe in the corner of Webster's office.

"Look at India—how small it seems. Well, if you skinned Earth and spread it out on the surface of Jupiter, it would look about as big as India does here."

There was a long silence while Webster contemplated the equation: Jupiter is to Earth as Earth is to India. Falcon had—deliberately, of course—chosen the best possible example . . .

Was it already ten years ago? Yes, it must have been. The crash lay seven years in the past (*that* date was engraved on his heart) and those initial tests had taken place three years before the first and last flight of the *Queen Elizabeth.*

Ten years ago, then, Commander (no, Lieutenant) Falcon had invited him to a preview—a three-day drift across the northern plains of India, within sight of the Himalayas. "Perfectly safe," he had promised. "It will get you away from the office—and will teach you what this whole thing is about."

Webster had not been disappointed. Next to his first journey to the Moon, it had been the most memorable experience of his life. And yet, as Falcon had assured him, it had been perfectly safe and quite uneventful.

They had taken off from Srinagar just before dawn, with the huge silver bubble of the balloon already catching the first light of the Sun. The ascent had been made in total silence; there were none of the roaring propane burners that had lifted the hot-air balloons of an earlier age. All the heat they needed came from the little pulsed-fusion reactor, weighing only a hundred

kilograms, hanging in the open mouth of the envelope. While they were climbing, its laser was zapping
ten times a second, igniting the merest whiff of
deuterium fuel; once they had reached altitude, it
would fire only a few times a minute, making up for
the heat lost through the great gasbag overhead.

And so, even while they were a kilometer above the
ground, they could hear dogs barking, people shout-
ing, bells ringing. Slowly the vast, Sun-smitten landscape expanded around them; two hours later, they
had leveled out at five kilometers and were taking
frequent draughts of oxygen. They could relax and
admire the scenery; the on-board instrumentation
was doing all the work—gathering the information
that would be required by the designers of the still-
unnamed liner of the skies.

It was a perfect day; the southwest monsoon would
not break for another month and there was hardly a
cloud in the sky. Time seemed to have come to a stop;
they resented the hourly radio reports that interrupted their reverie. And all around, to the horizon
and far beyond, was that infinite, ancient landscape
drenched with history—a patchwork of villages,
fields, temples, lakes, irrigation canals.

With a real effort, Webster broke the hypnotic spell
of that ten-year-old memory. It had converted him to
lighter-than-air flight—and it had made him realize
the enormous size of India, even in a world that could
be circled within ninety minutes. And yet, he repeated
to himself, Jupiter is to Earth as Earth is to India.

"Granted your argument," he said, "and supposing
the funds are available, there's another question you
have to answer. Why should you do better than

the—what is it—three hundred and twenty-six robot probes that have already made the trip?"

"I am better qualified than they were—as an observer and as a pilot. *Especially* as a pilot; don't forget—I've more experience of lighter-than-air flight than anyone in the world."

"You could still serve as controller and sit safely on Ganymede."

"But that's just the point! They've already done that. Don't you remember what killed the *Queen?"*

Webster knew perfectly well, but he merely answered, "Go on."

"Time lag—*time lag!* That idiot of a platform controller thought he was using a local radio circuit. But he'd been accidentally switched through a satellite—oh, maybe it wasn't his fault, but he should have noticed. That's a half-second time lag for the round trip. Even then it wouldn't have mattered, flying in calm air. It was the turbulence over the Grand Canyon that did it. When the platform tipped and he corrected for that—it had already tipped the other way. Ever tried to drive a car over a bumpy road with a half-second delay in the steering?"

"No, and I don't intend to try. But I can imagine it."

"Well, Ganymede is more than a million kilometers from Jupiter. That means a round-trip delay of six seconds. No, you need a controller on the spot—to handle emergencies in real time. Let me show you something. Mind if I use this?"

"Go ahead."

Falcon picked up a postcard that was lying on Webster's desk; they were almost obsolete on Earth, but this one showed a 3-D view of a Martian landscape and was decorated with exotic and expensive stamps. He held it so that it dangled vertically.

"This is an old trick but helps make my point. Place your thumb and finger on either side, not quite touching. That's right."

Webster put out his hand, almost but not quite gripping the card.

"Now catch it."

Falcon waited for a few seconds; then, without warning, he let go of the card. Webster's thumb and fingers closed on empty air.

"I'll do it again, just to show there's no deception. You see?"

Once again, the falling card slipped through Webster's fingers.

"Now you try it on me."

This time, Webster grasped the card and dropped it without warning. It had scarcely moved before Falcon had caught it; Webster almost imagined he could hear a click, so swift was the other's reaction.

"When they put me together again," Falcon remarked in an expressionless voice, "the surgeons made some improvements. This is one of them—and there are others. I want to make the most of them. Jupiter is the place where I can do it."

Webster stared for long seconds at the fallen card, absorbing the improbable colors of the Trivium Charontis Escarpment. Then he said quietly, "I understand. How long do you think it will take?"

"With your help, plus the bureau plus all the science foundations we can drag in—oh, three years. Then a year for trials—we'll have to send in at least two test models. So with luck—five years."

"That's about what I thought. I hope you get your

luck; you've earned it. But there's one thing I won't do."

"What's that?"

"Next time you go ballooning, don't expect *me* as passenger."

The World of the Gods

THE FALL FROM JUPITER V TO JUPITER ITSELF TAKES ONLY three and a half hours; few men could have slept on so awesome a journey. Sleep was a weakness that Howard Falcon hated, and the little he still required brought dreams that time had not yet been able to exorcise. But he could expect no rest in the three days that lay ahead and must seize what he could during the long fall down into that ocean of clouds, a hundred thousand kilometers below.

As soon as *Kon-Tiki* had entered her transfer orbit and all the computer checks were satisfactory, he prepared for the last sleep he might ever know. It seemed appropriate that at almost the same moment Jupiter eclipsed the bright and tiny Sun, he swept into the monstrous shadow of the planet. For a few minutes a strange, golden twilight enveloped the ship; then a quarter of the sky became an utterly black hole in space, while the rest was a blaze of stars. No matter how far one traveled across the Solar System, *they* never changed; these same constellations now shone on Earth, half a billion kilometers away. The only novelties here were the small, pale crescents of Callisto and Ganymede; doubtless there were a dozen other moons up there in the sky, but they were all much too tiny and too distant for the unaided eye to pick them out.

"Closing down for two hours," he reported to the mother ship, hanging a thousand kilometers above the desolate rocks of Jupiter V, in the radiation shadow of the tiny satellite. If it never served any other useful purpose, Jupiter V was a cosmetic bulldozer perpetually sweeping up the charged particles that made it unhealthy to linger close to Jupiter. Its wake was almost free of radiation, and here a ship could park in perfect safety while death sleeted invisibly all around.

Falcon switched on the sleep inducer and consciousness faded swiftly out as the electric pulses surged gently through his brain. While *Kon-Tiki* fell toward Jupiter, gaining speed second by second in that enormous gravitational field, he slept without dreams. They always came when he awoke; and he had brought his nightmares with him from Earth.

Yet he never dreamed of the crash itself, though he often found himself again face to face with that terrified superchimp, as he descended the spiral stairway between the collapsing gasbags. None of the simps had survived; those that were not killed outright were so badly injured that they had been painlessly euthed. He sometimes wondered why he dreamed only of this doomed creature, which he had never met before the last minutes of its life—and not of the friends and colleagues he had lost aboard the dying *Queen*.

The dreams he feared most always began with his first return to consciousness. There had been little physical pain; in fact, there had been no sensation of any kind. He was in darkness and silence and did not even seem to be breathing. And—strangest of all—he could not locate his limbs. He could move neither his hands nor his feet, because he did not know where they were.

The silence had been the first to yield. After hours or days, he had become aware of a faint throbbing and eventually, after long thought, he deduced that this was the beating of his own heart. That was the first of his many mistakes.

Then there had been faint pinpricks, sparkles of light, ghosts of pressures upon still unresponsive limbs. One by one his senses had returned, and pain had come with them. He had had to learn everything anew, recapitulating babyhood and infancy. Though his memory was unaffected and he could understand words that were spoken to him, it was months before he was able to answer except by the flicker of an eyelid. He could still remember the moments of triumph when he had spoken the first word, turned the page of a book—and, finally, learned to move under his own power. *That* was a victory, indeed, and it had taken him almost two years to prepare for it. A hundred times he had envied that dead superchimp, but *he* had been given no choice. The doctors had made their decision—and now, twelve years later, he was where no human being had ever traveled before and moving faster than any man in history.

Kon-Tiki was just emerging from shadow and the

Jovian dawn bridged the sky ahead in a titanic bow of light, when the persistent buzz of the alarm dragged Falcon up from sleep. The inevitable nightmares (he had been trying to summon a nurse but did not even have the strength to push the button) swiftly faded from consciousness; the greatest—and perhaps last—adventure of his life was before him.

He called Mission Control, now a hundred thousand kilometers away and falling swiftly below the curve of Jupiter, to report that everything was in order. His velocity had just passed fifty kilometers a second (*that* was one for the books) and in half an hour, *Kon-Tiki* would hit the outer fringes of the atmosphere, as he started on the most difficult entry in the entire Solar System. Although scores of probes had survived this flaming ordeal, they had been tough, solidly packed masses of instrumentation, able to withstand several hundred gravities of drag. *Kon-Tiki* would hit peaks of thirty *g* and would average more than ten before she came to rest in the upper reaches of the Jovian atmosphere. Very carefully and thoroughly, Falcon began to attach the elaborate system of restraints that anchored him to the walls of the cabin. When he had finished, he was virtually a part of the ship's structure.

The clock was counting backward; a hundred seconds to entry. For better or worse, he was committed. In a minute and a half, he would graze the Jovian atmosphere and would be caught irrevocably in the grip of the giant.

The countdown was three seconds late—not at all bad, considering the unknowns involved. Beyond the walls of the capsule came a ghostly sighing that rose steadily to a high-pitched, screaming roar. The noise was quite different from that of a re-entry on Earth or Mars; in this thin atmosphere of hydrogen and helium, all sounds were transformed a couple of octaves higher. On Jupiter, even thunder would have falsetto overtones.

With the rising scream came also mounting weight; within seconds, he was completely immobilized. His field of vision contracted until it embraced only the clock and the accelerometer; fifteen *g*, and 480 seconds to go.

He never lost consciousness; but then, he had not expected to. *Kon-Tiki*'s trail through the Jovian atmosphere must be really spectacular—by this time, thousands of kilometers long. Five hundred seconds after entry, the drag began to taper off: ten *g*, five *g*, two . . . Then weight vanished almost completely; he was falling free, all his enormous orbital velocity destroyed.

There was a sudden jolt as the incandescent remnants of the heat shield were jettisoned. It had done its work and would not be needed again; Jupiter could have it now. He released all but two of the restraining buckles and waited for the automatic sequencer to start the next and most critical series of events.

He did not see the first drogue parachute pop out, but he could feel the slight jerk and the rate of fall diminished immediately. *Kon-Tiki* had lost all her horizontal speed and was going straight down at a thousand kilometers an hour. Everything depended on the next sixty seconds.

There went the second drogue. He looked up through the overhead window and saw, to his immense relief, that clouds of glittering foil were billowing out behind the falling ship. Like a great flower unfurling, the thousands of cubic meters of the balloon spread out across the sky, scooping up the thin gas until it was fully inflated. *Kon-Tiki*'s rate of fall dropped to a few kilometers an hour and remained constant. Now there was plenty of time; it would take him days to fall all the way down to the surface of Jupiter.

But he would get there eventually, if he did nothing about it; the balloon overhead was merely acting as an efficient parachute. It was providing no lift, nor could it do so while the gas inside and out was the same.

With its characteristic and rather disconcerting crack, the fusion reactor started up, pouring torrents of heat into the envelope overhead. Within five minutes, the rate of fall had become zero; within six, the ship had started to rise. According to the radar altimeter, it had leveled out at 430 kilometers above the surface—or whatever passed for a surface on Jupiter.

Only one kind of balloon will work in an atmosphere of hydrogen, which is the lightest of all gases—and that is a hot-hydrogen balloon. As long as the fusor kept ticking over, Falcon could remain aloft, drifting across a world that could hold a hundred Pacifics. After traveling more than half a billion kilometers, *Kon-Tiki* had at last begun to justify her name. She was an aerial raft, adrift upon the current of the Jovian atmosphere.

Though a whole new world was lying around him, it was more than a hour before Falcon could examine the view. First he had to check all the capsule's systems and test its response to the controls. He had to learn how much extra heat was necessary to produce a

desired rate of ascent and how much gas he must vent
in order to descend. Above all, there was the question
of stability. He must adjust the length of the cables
attaching his capsule to the huge, pear-shaped balloon, to damp out vibrations and get the smoothest
possible ride. So far, he was lucky; at this level, the
wind was steady and the Doppler reading on the
invisible surface gave him a ground speed of 350
kilometers an hour. For Jupiter, that was modest;
winds of up to a thousand had been observed. But
mere speed, of course, was unimportant; the real
danger was turbulence. If he ran into that, only skill
and experience and swift reaction could save him—
and these were not matters that could yet be pro-
grammed into a computer.

Not until he was satisfied that he had got the feel of
this strange craft did Falcon pay any attention to
Mission Control's pleadings. Then he deployed the
booms carrying the instrumentation and the atmospheric samplers; the capsule now resembled a rather
untidy Christmas tree but still rode rode smoothly
down the Jovian winds, while it radioed up its torrents of information to the recorders on the ship a
hundred thousand kilometers above. And now, at last,
he could look around.

His first impression was unexpected and even a
little disappointing. As far as the scale of things was
concerned, he might have been ballooning over an
ordinary cloudscape on Earth. The horizon seemed at
a normal distance; there was no feeling at all that he
was on a world eleven times the diameter of his own.
Then he looked at the infrared radar, sounding the
layers of atmosphere beneath him—and knew how
badly his eyes had been deceived.

That layer of clouds, apparently five kilometers away, was really sixty kilometers below. And the horizon, whose distance he would have guessed at two hundred, was actually three thousand kilometers from the ship.

The crystalline clarity of the hydro-helium atmosphere and the enormous curvature of the planet had fooled him completely. It was even harder to judge distances here than on the Moon; everything he saw must be multiplied by ten.

It was a simple matter and he should have been prepared for it. Yet somehow it disturbed him profoundly. He did not feel that Jupiter was huge but that *he* had shrunk—to a tenth of his normal size. Perhaps, with time, he would grow accustomed to the inhuman scale of this world; yet as he stared toward that unbelievably distant horizon, he felt as if a wind colder than the atmosphere around him was blowing through his soul. Despite all his arguments, this might never be a place for man. He could well be both the first and the last to descend through the clouds of Jupiter.

The sky above was almost black, except for a few wisps of ammonia cirrus perhaps twenty kilometers overhead. It was cold up there on the fringes of space, but both pressure and temperature increased rapidly with depth. At the level where *Kon-Tiki* was drifting now, it was fifty degrees centigrade below zero and the pressure was five atmospheres. A hundred kilometers farther down, it would be as warm as equatorial Earth—and the pressure about the same as at the bottom of one of the shallower seas. Ideal conditions for life.

A quarter of the brief Jovian day had already gone;

the Sun was halfway up the sky, but the light on the unbroken cloudscape below had a curious mellow quality. That extra half billion kilometers had robbed the Sun of all its power; though the sky was clear, Falcon found himself continually thinking that it was a heavily overcast day. When night fell, the onset of darkness would be swift, indeed; though it was still morning, there was a sense of autumnal twilight in the air. But autumn, of course, was something that never came to Jupiter. There were no seasons here.

Kon-Tiki had come down in the exact center of the Equatorial Zone—the least colorful part of the planet. The sea of clouds that stretched out to the horizon was tinted a pale salmon; there were none of the yellows and pinks and even reds that banded Jupiter at higher latitudes. The Great Red Spot itself—most spectacular of all the planet's features—lay thousands of kilometers to the south. It had been a temptation to descend there, but the South Tropical Disturbance was unusually active, with currents reaching fifteen hundred kilometers an hour. It would have been asking for trouble to head into that maelstrom of unknown forces. The Great Red Spot and its mysteries would have to wait for future expeditions.

The Sun, moving across the sky twice as swiftly as it did on Earth, was now nearing the zenith and had become eclipsed by the great silver canopy of the balloon. *Kon-Tiki* was still drifting swiftly, smoothly westward at a steady 350, but only the radar gave any indication of this. Was it always as calm here? Falcon asked himself. The scientists who had talked learnedly of the Jovian doldrums and had predicted that the equator would be the quietest place seemed to know what they were talking about, after all. He had been profoundly skeptical of all such forecasts and had agreed with one unusually modest researcher who had told him bluntly, "There are *no* experts on Jupiter." Well, there would be at least one by the end of this day.

If he managed to survive until then.

The Voices of the Deep

THAT FIRST DAY, THE FATHER OF THE GODS SMILED UPON him. It was as calm and peaceful here on Jupiter as it had been, years ago, when he was drifting with Webster across the plains of northern India. Falcon had time to master his new skills, until *Kon-Tiki* seemed an extension of his own body. Such luck was more than he had dared hope and he began to wonder what price he might have to pay for it.

The five hours of daylight were almost over; the clouds below were full of shadows, which gave them a massive solidity they had not possessed when the Sun was higher. Color was swiftly draining from the sky, except in the west itself, where a band of deepening purple lay along the horizon. Above this band was the thin crescent of a closer moon, pale and bleached against the utter blackness beyond.

With a speed perceptible to the eye, the Sun went straight down over the edge of Jupiter, three thousand kilometers away. The stars came out in their legions— and there was the beautiful evening star of Earth, on the very frontier of twilight, reminding him how far he was from home. It followed the Sun down into the west; man's first night on Jupiter had begun.

With the onset of darkness, *Kon-Tiki* started to sink. The balloon was no longer heated by the feeble sunlight and was losing a small part of its buoyancy. Falcon did nothing to increase lift; he had expected this and was planning to descend.

The invisible cloud deck was still fifty kilometers below and he would reach it about midnight. It showed up clearly on the infrared radar, which also reported that it contained a vast array of complex carbon compounds, as well as the usual hydrogen, helium and ammonia. The chemists were dying for samples of that fluffy, pinkish stuff; though some atmospheric probes had already gathered a few grams, that had only whetted their appetites. Half the basic molecules of life were here, floating high above the surface of Jupiter. And where there was food, could life be far away? That was the question that, after more than a hundred years, no one had been able to answer.

The infrared was blocked by the clouds, but the microwave radar sliced right through and showed layer after layer, all the way down to the hidden surface more than four hundred kilometers below. That was barred to him by enormous pressures and temperatures; not even robot probes had ever reached it intact. It lay in tantalizing inaccessibility at the bottom of the radar screen, slightly fuzzy and showing a curious granular structure that his equipment could not resolve.

An hour after sunset, he dropped his first probe. It fell swiftly for a hundred kilometers, then began to float in the denser atmosphere, sending back torrents of radio signals, which he relayed up to Mission Control. Then there was nothing else to do until sunrise, except to keep an eye on the rate of descent, monitor the instruments and answer occasional queries. While she was drifting in this steady current, *Kon-Tiki* could look after herself.

Just before midnight, a woman controller came on watch and introduced herself with the usual pleasantries. Ten minutes later, she called again, her voice at once serious and excited.

"Howard! Listen in on channel forty-six—high gain."

Channel 46? There were so many telemetering circuits that he knew the numbers of only those that were critical; but as soon as he threw the switch, he recognized this one. He was plugged into the microphone on the probe, floating 130 kilometers below him in an atmosphere now almost as dense as water.

At first, there was only a soft hiss of whatever strange winds stirred down in the darkness of that unimaginable world. And then, out of the background noise, there slowly emerged a booming vibration that grew louder and louder, like the beating of a gigantic drum. It was so low that it was felt as much as heard and the beats steadily increased their tempo, though the pitch never changed. Now it was a swift, almost infrasonic throbbing—and then, suddenly, in mid-vibration, it stopped, so abruptly that the mind could not accept the silence, but memory continued to manufacture a ghostly echo in the deepest caverns of the brain.

It was the most extraordinary sound that Falcon had ever heard, even among the multitudinous noises of Earth. He could think of no natural phenomenon that could have caused it, nor was it like the cry of any animal, not even one of the great whales.

It came again, following exactly the same pattern. Now that he was prepared for it, he estimated the length of the sequence; from first faint throb to final crescendo, it lasted just over ten seconds.

And this time, there was a real echo, very faint and far away. Perhaps it came from one of the many reflecting layers deeper in this stratified atmosphere; perhaps it was another more distant source. Falcon waited for a second echo, but it never came.

Mission Control reacted quickly and asked him to drop another probe at once. With two microphones operating, it would be possible to find the approximate location of the sources. Oddly enough, none of *Kon-Tiki*'s own external mikes could detect anything except wind noises; the boomings, whatever they were, must have been trapped and channeled beneath an atmospheric reflecting layer far below.

They were coming, it was soon discovered, from a cluster of sources about two thousand kilometers away. The distance gave no indication of their power; in Earth's oceans, quite feeble sounds could travel equally far. And as for the obvious assumption that living creatures were responsible, the chief exobiologist quickly ruled that out.

"I'll be very disappointed," said Dr. Brenner, "if there are no microorganisms or plants here. But nothing like animals, because there's no free oxygen.

All biochemical reactions on Jupiter must be low-energy ones—there's just no way an active creature could generate enough power to function."

Falcon wondered if this were true; he had heard the argument before and reserved judgment.

"In any case," continued Brenner, "some of those sound waves are a hundred meters long! Even an animal as big as a whale couldn't produce them. They *must* have a natural origin."

Yes, that seemed plausible, and probably the physicists would be able to come up with an explanation. What would a blind alien make, Falcon wondered, of the sounds he might hear when standing beside a stormy sea or a geyser or a volcano or a waterfall? He might well attribute them to some huge beast.

About an hour before sunrise, the voices of the deep died away and Falcon began to busy himself with preparation for the dawn of his second day. *Kon-Tiki* was now only five kilometers above the nearest cloud layer; the external pressure had risen to ten atmospheres and the temperature was a tropical thirty degrees. A man could be comfortable here with no more equipment than a breathing mask and the right grade of heliox mixture.

"We've some good news for you," Mission Control reported soon after dawn. "The cloud layer's breaking up. You'll have partial clearing in an hour—but watch out for turbulence."

"I've already noticed some," Falcon answered. "How far down will I be able to see?"

"At least twenty kilometers, down to the second thermocline. *That* cloud deck is solid—it never breaks."

And it's out of my reach, Falcon told himself; the

temperature down there must be over a hundred degrees. This was the first time that any balloonist had ever had to worry not about his ceiling but about his—basement?

Ten minutes later, he could see what Mission Control had already observed from its superior vantage point. There was a change in color near the horizon and the cloud layer had become ragged and humpy, as if something had torn it open. He turned up his little nuclear furnace and gave *Kon-Tiki* another five kilometers of altitude so that he could get a better view.

The sky below was clearing rapidly—completely, as if something was dissolving away the solid overcast. An abyss was opening up before his eyes; a moment later, he sailed out over the edge of a cloud canyon twenty kilometers deep and a thousand kilometers wide.

A new world lay spread beneath him; Jupiter had stripped away one of its many veils. The second layer of clouds, unattainably far below, was much darker in color than the first. It was almost salmon pink and curiously mottled with little islands of brick red. They were all oval-shaped, with their long axes pointing east–west, in the direction of the prevailing wind. There were hundreds of them, all about the same size, and they reminded Falcon of puffy little cumulus clouds in the terrestrial sky.

He reduced buoyancy and *Kon-Tiki* began to drop down the face of the dissolving cliff. It was then that he noticed the snow.

White flakes were forming in the air and drifting slowly downward. Yet it was much too warm for snow—and, in any event, there was scarcely a trace of water at this altitude. Moreover, there was no glitter nor sparkle about these flakes as they went cascading down into the depths; when, presently, a few landed on an instrument boom outside the main viewing port, he saw that they were a dull, opaque white—not crystalline at all—and quite large, several centimeters across. They looked like wax and Falcon guessed that this was precisely what they were. Some chemical reaction was taking place in the atmosphere around him, condensing out the hydrocarbons floating in the Jovian air.

A hundred kilometers ahead, a disturbance was taking place in the cloud layer. The little red ovals were being jostled around and were beginning to form a spiral—the familiar cyclonic pattern so common in the meteorology of Earth. The vortex was emerging with astonishing speed; if that was a storm ahead, Falcon told himself, he was in big trouble.

And then his concern changed to wonder—and to fear. For what was developing in his line of flight was not a storm at all. Something enormous—something scores of kilometers across—was rising through the clouds.

The reassuring thought that it, too, might be a cloud—a thunderhead boiling up from the lower levels of the atmosphere—lasted only a few seconds. No; this was *solid*. It shouldered its way through the pink-and-salmon overcast like an iceberg rising from the deeps.

An *iceberg*, floating on hydrogen? That was impossible, of course; but perhaps it was not too remote an analogy. As soon as he focused the telescope upon the enigma, Falcon saw that it was a whitish mass, threaded with streaks of red and brown. It must be, he decided, the same stuff as the "snowflakes" falling around him—a mountain range of wax. And it was not, he soon realized, as solid as he had thought; around the edges, it was continually crumbling and reforming.

"I know what it is," he radioed Mission Control, which for the past few minutes had been asking anxious questions. "It's a mass of bubbles—some kind of foam. Hydrocarbon froth. Get the chemists working on—*just a minute!"*

"What is it?" called Mission Control. "What is it?"

He ignored the frantic pleas from space and concentrated all his mind upon the image in the telescope field. He had to be sure; if he made a mistake, he would be the laughingstock of the Solar System.

Then he relaxed, glanced at the clock and switched off the nagging voice from Jupiter V.

"Hello, Mission Control," he said very formally. "This is Howard Falcon aboard *Kon-Tiki*, Ephemeris Time Nineteen Hours Twenty-One Minutes Fifteen Seconds. Latitude Zero Degrees Five Minutes North. Longitude One Hundred Five Degrees Forty-Two Minutes, System One.

"Tell Dr. Brenner that there is life on Jupiter. And it's *big."*

The Wheels of Poseidon

"I'M VERY HAPPY TO BE PROVED WRONG," DR. BRENNER radioed back cheerfully. "Nature always has something up her sleeve. Keep the long-focus camera on target and give us the steadiest pictures you can."

The things moving up and down those waxen slopes were still too far away for Falcon to make out many details, and they must have been very large to be visible at all at such a distance. Almost black and shaped like arrowheads, they maneuvered by slow undulations of their entire bodies, so that they looked rather like giant manta rays swimming above some tropical reef.

Perhaps they were sky-borne cattle browsing on the cloud pastures of Jupiter, for they seemed to be feeding along the dark, red-brown streaks that ran like dried-up river beds down the flanks of the floating cliffs. Occasionally, one of them would dive headlong into the mountain of foam and disappear completely from sight.

Kon-Tiki was moving only slowly with respect to the cloud layer below; it would be at least three hours before she was above those ephemeral hills. She was in a race with the Sun; Falcon hoped that darkness would not fall before he could get a good view of the mantas, as he had christened them, as well as the fragile landscape over which they flapped their way.

It was a long three hours; during the whole time, he kept the external microphones on full gain, wondering if here was the source of that booming in the night. The mantas were certainly large enough to have produced it; when he could get an accurate measurement, he discovered that they were almost a hundred meters across the wings. That was three times the length of the largest whale—though he doubted if they could weigh more than a few tons.

Half an hour before sunset, *Kon-Tiki* was almost above the "mountains."

"No," said Falcon, answering Mission Control's repeated questions about the mantas. "They're still showing no reaction to me. I don't think they're intelligent—they look like harmless vegetarians. And even if they try to chase me—I'm sure they can't reach my altitude."

Yet he was a little disappointed when the mantas showed not the slightest interest in him as he sailed high above their feeding ground. Perhaps they had no way of detecting his presence; when he examined and photographed them through the telescope, he could see no signs of any sense organs. The creatures were merely huge black deltas rippling over hills and valleys that, in reality, were little more substantial than the clouds of Earth. Though they looked so solid, Falcon knew that anyone who stepped on those white mountains would go crashing through them as if they were made of tissue paper.

At close quarters, he could see the myriads of cellules or bubbles from which they were formed. Some of these were quite large—a meter or so in diameter—and Falcon wondered in what witch's caldron of hydrocarbons they had been brewed. There must be enough petrochemicals deep down in the atmosphere of Jupiter to supply all Earth's needs for a million years.

The short day had almost gone when he passed over the crest of the waxen hills and the light was fading rapidly along their lower slopes. There were no mantas on this western side and for some reason, the topography was very different. The foam was sculpted into long, level terraces, like the interior of a lunar crater. He could almost imagine that they were gigantic steps leading down to the hidden surface of the planet.

And on the lowest of those steps, just clear of the swirling clouds that the mountain had displaced when it came surging skyward, was a roughly oval mass two or three kilometers across. It was difficult to see, being only a little darker than the gray-white foam on which it rested. Falcon's first reaction was that he was looking at a forest of pallid trees, like giant mushrooms that had never seen the Sun.

Yes, it must be a forest—he could see hundreds of thin trunks springing from the white, waxy froth in which they were rooted. But the trees were packed astonishingly close together; there was scarcely any space between them. Perhaps it was not a forest after all but a single enormous tree—like one of the giant, multiple-trunked banyans of the East. He had once seen, in Java, a banyan tree two hundred meters across; this monster was at least ten times that size.

The light had almost gone; the cloudscape had turned purple with refracted sunlight and in a few seconds that, too, would have vanished. In the very last light of his second day on Jupiter, Howard Falcon saw—or thought he saw—something that cast the very gravest doubts on his interpretation of the white oval.

Unless the dim light had totally deceived him, those hundreds of thin trunks were beating back and forth, in perfect synchronism, like fronds of kelp rocking in the surge.

And the tree was no longer in the place where he had first seen it.

"Sorry about this," said Mission Control soon after sunset, "but we think Source Beta is going to blow within the next hour. Probability seventy percent."

Falcon glanced quickly at the chart. Beta—Jupiter latitude 140 degrees—was thirty thousand kilometers away and well below his horizon. Even though major eruptions ran as high as ten megatons, he was much too far away for the shock wave to be a serious danger. The radio storm that it would trigger was, however, quite a different matter.

The decameter outbursts that sometimes made Jupiter the most powerful radio source in the whole sky had been discovered back in the 1950s, to the utter astonishment of the astronomers. Now, more than a century later, their real cause was still a mystery. Only the symptoms were understood; the explanation was completely unknown.

The "volcano" theory had best stood the test of time—although no one imagined that this word had the same meaning on Jupiter as on Earth. At frequent intervals—often several times a day—titanic eruptions occurred in the lower depths of the atmosphere, probably on the hidden surface of the planet itself. A great column of gas, more than a thousand kilometers high, would start boiling upward, as if determined to escape into space.

Against the most powerful gravitational field of all the planets, it had no chance. Yet some traces—a mere few million tons—usually managed to reach the Jovian ionosphere; and when they did, all hell broke loose.

The radiation belts surrounding Jupiter completely dwarf the feeble Van Allen belts of Earth. When they are short-circuited by an ascending column of gas, the result is an electrical discharge millions of times more powerful than any terrestrial flash of lightning; it sends a colossal thunderclap of radio noise flooding across the entire Solar System—and on out to the stars.

It had been discovered that these radio outbursts came from four main areas of the planet; perhaps there were weaknesses here that allowed the fires of the interior to break out from time to time. The scientists on Ganymede, largest of Jupiter's many moons, now thought that they could predict the onset of a decameter storm; their accuracy was about as good as a weather forecaster's of the early 1900s.

Falcon did not know whether to welcome or to fear a radio storm; it would certainly add to the value of the mission—if he survived it. His course had been planned to keep as far as possible from the main centers of disturbance, especially the most active one, Source Alpha. As luck would have it, the threatening Beta was the closest to him; he hoped that thirty thousand kilometers—almost the circumference of Earth—was a safe enough distance.

"Probability ninety percent," said Mission Control with a distinct note of urgency. "And forget that hour. Ganymede says it may be any moment."

The radio had scarcely fallen silent when the reading on the magnetic-field-strength meter started to shoot upward. Before it could go off-scale, it reversed and began to drop as rapidly as it had risen. Far away and thousands of kilometers below, something had given the planet's molten core a titanic jolt.

"There she blows!" called Mission Control.

"Thanks—I already know. When will the storm hit me?"

"You can expect onset in five minutes. Peak in ten."

Far round the curve of Jupiter, a funnel of gas as wide as the Pacific Ocean was climbing spaceward at thousands of kilometers an hour. Already, the thunderstorms of the lower atmosphere would be raging around it—but they were as nothing to the fury that would explode when the radiation belt was reached and it began dumping its surplus electrons onto the planet. Falcon began to retract all the instrument booms that were extended out from the capsule; there were no other precautions he could take. It would be four hours before the atmospheric shock wave reached him—but the radio blast, traveling at the speed of light, would be here in a tenth of a second once the discharge had been triggered.

The radio monitor, scanning back and forth across the spectrum, still showed nothing unusual—just the normal mush of background static. Then Falcon noticed that the noise level was slowly creeping upward. The explosion was gathering its strength.

At such a distance, he had never expected to *see* anything. But suddenly a flicker as of far-off heat lightning danced along the eastern horizon. Simultaneously, half the circuit breakers jumped out of the main switchboard, the lights failed and all communications channels went dead.

He tried to move but was completely unable to do so. The paralysis that gripped him was not merely psychological; he seemed to have lost all control of his limbs and could feel a painful tingling sensation over his entire body. It was impossible that the electric field could have penetrated into this shielded cabin—yet there was a flickering glow over the instrument board and he could hear the unmistakable crackle of a brush discharge.

With a series of sharp bangs, the emergency systems operated and the overloads reset themselves. The lights flickered on again and Falcon's paralysis disappeared as swiftly as it had come. After glancing at the board to make sure that all circuits were back to normal, he moved quickly to the viewing ports.

There was no need to switch on the inspection lamps—the cables supporting the capsule seemed to be on fire. Lines of light, glowing an electric blue against the darkness, stretched upward from the main lift ring to the equator of the giant balloon; and rolling slowly along several of them were dazzling balls of fire.

The sight was so strange and so beautiful that it was

hard to read any menace in it. Few people, Falcon knew, had ever seen ball lighting from such close quarters—and certainly none had survived if they were riding a hydrogen-filled balloon back in the atmosphere of Earth. He remembered the flaming death of the _Hindenburg,_ destroyed by a stray spark when she docked at Lakehurst in 1937; as it had done so often in the past, the horrifying old newsreel film flashed through his mind. But at least that could not happen here, though there was more hydrogen above his head than had ever filled the last of the zeppelins. It would be a few billion years yet before anyone could light a fire in the atmosphere of Jupiter.

With a sound like briskly frying bacon, the speech circuit came back to life.

"Hello, _Kon-Tiki_—are you receiving? Are you receiving?"

The words were chopped and badly distorted but intelligible. Falcon's spirits lifted; he had resumed contact with the world of men.

"I receive you," he said. "Quite an electrical display, but no damage—so far."

"Thanks—thought we'd lost you. Please check telemetry channels three, seven, twenty-six. Also gain on camera two. And we don't quite believe the readings on the external ionization probes."

Reluctantly, Falcon tore his gaze away from the fascinating pyrotechnic display around _Kon-Tiki,_ though from time to time he kept glancing out the windows. The ball lightning disappeared first, the fiery globes slowly expanding until they reached a critical size, at which they vanished in a gentle explosion. But for an hour later, there were still faint glows around all the exposed metal on the outside of the capsule; and the radio circuits remained noisy until well after midnight.

The remaining hours of darkness were completely uneventful—until just before dawn. Because it came from the east, Falcon assumed that he was seeing the first faint hint of sunrise. Then he realized that it was still twenty minutes too early for it—and the glow that had appeared along the horizon was moving toward him even as he watched. It swiftly detached itself from the arch of stars that marked the invisible edge of the planet and he saw that it was a relatively narrow band, quite sharply defined. The beam of an enormous searchlight appeared to be swinging beneath the clouds.

Perhaps a hundred kilometers behind the first racing bar of light came another, parallel to it and moving at the same speed. And beyond that another, and another—until all the sky flickered with alternating sheets of light and darkness.

By this time, Falcon thought, he had been inured to wonders and it seemed impossible that this display of pure, soundless luminosity could present the slightest danger. But it was so astonishing and so inexplicable that he felt cold naked fear gnawing at his self-control. No man could look upon such a sight without feeling a helpless pygmy, in the presence of forces beyond his comprehension. Was it possible that, after all, Jupiter carried not only life but intelligence? And, perhaps, an intelligence that only now was beginning to react to his alien presence.

"Yes, we see it," said Mission Control in a voice that echoed his own awe. "We've no idea what it is. Stand by—we're calling Ganymede."

The display was slowly fading; the bands racing in

from the far horizon were much fainter, as if the energies that powered them were becoming exhausted. In five minutes, it was all over; the last faint pulse of light flickered along the western sky and then was gone. Its passing left Falcon with an overwhelming sense of relief. The sight was so hypnotic and so disturbing that it was not good for any man's peace of mind to contemplate it too long.

He was more shaken than he cared to admit. The electrical storm was something that he could understand, but *this* was totally incomprehensible.

Mission Control was still silent. Falcon knew that the information banks up on Ganymede were now being searched while men and computers turned their minds to the problem. If no answer could be found there, it would be necessary to call Earth; that would mean a delay of almost an hour. The possibility that even Earth might be unable to help was one that Falcon did not care to contemplate.

He had never before been so glad to hear the voice of Mission Control as when Dr. Brenner finally came on the circuit. The biologist sounded relieved—yet subdued, like a man who had just come through some great intellectual crisis.

"Hello, *Kon-Tiki*. We've solved your problem, but we can still hardly believe it.

"What you've been seeing is bioluminescence— very similar to that produced by microorganisms in the tropical seas of Earth. Here they're in the atmosphere, not the ocean, but the principle is the same."

"But the pattern," protested Falcon. "It was so regular—so *artificial*. And it was hundreds of kilometers across!"

"It was even larger than you imagine—you ob-

served only a small part of it. The whole pattern was
five thousand kilometers wide and looked like a
revolving wheel. You merely saw the spokes, sweeping
past you at about a kilometer a second—"

"A *second*," Falcon could not help interjecting. "No
animals could move that fast!"

"Of course not—let me explain. What you saw was
triggered by the shock wave from Source Beta, moving
at the speed of sound."

"But what about the pattern?" Falcon insisted.

"That's the surprising part. It's a very rare phenomenon, but identical wheels of light—except that
they're a thousand times smaller—have been observed in the Persian Gulf and the Indian Ocean.
Listen to this: British India Company's Patna, Persian
Gulf, May 1880, eleven-thirty P.M.—'An enormous
luminous wheel, whirling round, the spokes of which
appeared to brush the ship along. The spokes were two
hundred or three hundred yards long . . . each wheel
contained about sixteen spokes . . .' And here's one
from the Gulf of Oman, dated 23 May, 1906: 'The
intensely bright luminescence approached us rapidly,
shooting sharply defined light rays to the west in rapid
succession, like the beam from the searchlight of a
warship. . . . To the left of us, a gigantic fiery wheel
formed itself, with spokes that reached as far as one
could see. The whole wheel whirled around for two or
three minutes.' The archive computer on Ganymede
dug up about five hundred cases—it would have
printed out the lot if we hadn't stopped it in time."

"I'm convinced—but still baffled."

"I don't blame you; the full explanation wasn't
worked out until late in the twentieth century. It
seems that these luminous wheels are the results of

submarine earthquakes and always occur in shallow waters, where the shock waves can be reflected and cause standard wave patterns. Sometimes bars— sometimes rotating wheels—the 'Wheels of Poseidon,' they've been called. The theory was finally proved by making underwater explosions and photographing the results from a satellite. No wonder sailors used to be superstitious. Who would have believed a thing like *this*?"

So that was it, Falcon told himself. When Source Beta blew its top, it must have sent shock waves in all directions—through the compressed gas of the lower atmosphere, through the solid body of Jupiter itself. Meeting and crisscrossing, those waves must have canceled here, reinforced there; the whole planet must have rung like a bell.

Yet the explanation did not destroy the sense of wonder and awe; he would never be able to forget those flickering bands of light racing through the unattainable depths of the Jovian atmosphere. He felt that he was not merely on a strange planet but in some magical realm between myth and reality.

This was a world where absolutely *anything* could happen and no man could possibly guess what the future would bring.

And he still had a whole day to go.

Medusa

WHEN THE TRUE DAWN FINALLY ARRIVED, IT BROUGHT A sudden change of weather. *Kon-Tiki* was moving through a blizzard; waxen snowflakes were falling so thickly that visibility was reduced to zero. Falcon began to worry about the weight that might be accumulating on the envelope; then he noticed that any flakes settling outside the windows quickly disappeared. *Kon-Tiki*'s continuous outpouring of heat was evaporating them as swiftly as they arrived.

If he had been ballooning on Earth, he would also have worried about the possibility of collision. That, at least, was no danger here; any Jovian mountains were several hundred kilometers below him. And as for the floating islands of foam, hitting them would probably be like plowing into slightly hardened soap bubbles.

Nevertheless, he switched on the horizontal radar,

which until now had been completely useless; only the vertical beam, giving his distance from the invisible surface, so far had been of any value. And then he had another surprise.

Scattered across a huge sector of the sky ahead were dozens of large and brilliant echoes. They were completely isolated from one another and hung apparently unsupported in space. Falcon suddenly remembered a phrase that earliest aviators had used to describe one of the hazards of their profession—"clouds stuffed with rocks." That was a perfect description of what seemed to lie in the track of *Kon-Tiki*.

It was a disconcerting sight; then Falcon again reminded himself that nothing *really* solid could possibly hover in this atmosphere. Perhaps it was some strange meteorological phenomenon—and, in any case, the nearest echo was over two hundred kilometers away.

He reported to Mission Control, which could provide no explanation. But it gave the welcome news that he would be clear of the blizzard in another thirty minutes.

It did not warn him, however, of the violent cross wind that abruptly grabbed *Kon-Tiki* and swept it almost at right angles to its previous track. Falcon needed all his skill and the maximum use of what little control he had over his ungainly vehicle to prevent it from being capsized. Within minutes, he was racing northward at five hundred kilometers an hour; then, as suddenly as it had started, the turbulence ceased; he was still moving at high speed but in smooth air. He wondered if he had been caught in the Jovian equivalent of a jet stream.

Then the snowstorm suddenly dissolved and he saw what Jupiter had been preparing for him.

Kon-Tiki had entered the funnel of a gigantic whirlpool, at least three hundred kilometers across. The balloon was being swept along a curving wall of cloud; overhead, the Sun was shining in a clear sky, but far beneath, this great hole in the atmosphere drilled down to unknown depths, until it reached a misty floor where lightning flickered almost continuously.

Though the vessel was being dragged downward so slowly that it was in no immediate danger, Falcon increased the flow of heat into the envelope, until *Kon-Tiki* hovered at a constant altitude. Not until then did he abandon the fantastic spectacle outside and consider again the problem of the radar.

The nearest echo was now only forty kilometers away—and all of them, he quickly realized, were distributed along the wall of the vortex; they were moving with it, apparently caught in the whirlpool like *Kon-Tiki* itself. He aimed the telescope along the radar bearing and found himself looking at a curious mottled cloud that almost filled the field of view.

It was not easy to see, being only little darker than the whirling wall of mist that formed its background. Not until he had been staring for several minutes did Falcon realize that he had met it once before.

The first time, it had been crawling across the drifting mountains of foam and he had mistaken it for a giant, many-trunked tree. Now at last he could appreciate its real size and complexity and he could give it a better name to fix its image in his mind. It did not resemble a tree at all but a jellyfish—a medusa, such as might be met trailing its tentacles as it drifted along the warm eddies of the Gulf Stream.

This medusa was two kilometers across and its scores of dangling tentacles were hundreds of meters long. They swayed slowly back and forth in perfect unison, taking more than a minute for each complete undulation—almost as if the creature were clumsily rowing itself through the sky.

The other echoes were more distant medusae; Falcon turned the telescope on half a dozen and could see no variations in shape or size. They all seemed to be of the same species and he wondered just why they were drifting lazily around in this thousand-kilometer orbit. Perhaps they were feeding upon the aerial plankton sucked in by the whirlpool—as *Kon-Tiki* itself had been.

"Do you realize, Howard," said Dr. Brenner when he had recovered from his initial astonishment, "that this thing is about a hundred thousand times as large as the biggest whale? And even if it's only a gasbag, it must still weigh a million tons! I can't even guess at its metabolism; it must generate megawatts of heat to maintain its buoyancy."

"But if it's just a gasbag, why is it such a damn good radar reflector?"

"I haven't the faintest idea. Can you get any closer?"

Brenner's question was not an idle one; if Falcon changed altitude to take advantage of the differing wind velocities, he could approach the medusa as closely as he wished. At the moment, he preferred his present forty kilometers and said so, firmly.

"I see what you mean," Brenner answered a little reluctantly. "Let's stay where we are for the present." That "we" gave Falcon a certain wry amusement; an

extra hundred thousand kilometers made a considerable difference to one's point of view.

For the next two hours, *Kon-Tiki* drifted unevent-
fully in the gyre of the great whirlpool, while Falcon
experimented with filters and camera contrast, trying
to get a clear view of the medusa. He began to wonder
if its elusive coloration were some kind of camouflage;
perhaps, like many animals of Earth, it was trying to
lose itself against its background. That was a trick
used both by hunters and by the hunted.

In which category was the medusa? That was a
question he could hardly expect to have answered in
the short time that was left to him. Yet just before
noon, without the slightest warning, the answer came.

Like a squadron of antique jet fighters, five mantas
came sweeping through the wall of mist that formed
the funnel of the vortex. They were flying in a V
formation, directly toward the pallid gray cloud of the
medusa—and there was no doubt, in Falcon's mind,
that they were on the attack. He had been quite wrong
to assume that they were harmless vegetarians.

Yet everything happened at such a leisurely pace
that it was like watching a slow-motion film. The
mantas undulated along at perhaps fifty kilometers an
hour; it seemed ages before they reached the medusa,
which continued to paddle imperturbably along at an
even slower speed. Huge though they were, the mantas
looked tiny beside the monster they were approach-
ing; when they flapped down onto its back, they
appeared about as large as birds landing on a whale.

Could the medusa defend itself? Falcon wondered.
As long as they avoided those huge, clumsy tentacles,
he did not see how the attacking mantas could be in

any danger. And perhaps their host was not even
aware of them; they could be insignificant parasites, as
tolerated as fleas upon a dog.

But now it was obvious that the medusa was in
distress. With agonizing slowness, it began to tip over,
like a capsizing ship. After ten minutes, it had tilted
forty-five degrees; it was also rapidly losing altitude. It
was impossible not to feel a sense of pity for the
beleaguered monster, and to Howard Falcon the sight
brought bitter memories. In a grotesque way, the fall
of the medusa was almost a parody of the dying
Queen's last moments.

Yet he knew that his sympathies were on the wrong
side. High intelligence could only develop among
predators—not among the drifting browsers of either
sea or air. The mantas were far closer to him than was
this monstrous bag of gas; and anyway, who could
really sympathize with a creature a hundred thousand
times larger than a whale?

Then he noticed that the medusa's tactics seemed to
be having some effect. The mantas had been disturbed
by its slow roll and were flapping heavily away from its
back—like gorged vultures interrupted at mealtime.
But they did not move very far, continuing to hover a
few meters from the still capsizing monster.

There was a sudden, blinding flash of light, synchro-
nized with a crash of static over the radio. One of the
mantas, slowly twisting end over end, was plummet-
ing straight downward. As it fell, it trailed behind it a
smoky black plume. Though there could be no fire, the
resemblance to an aircraft going down in flames was
quiet uncanny.

In unison, the remaining mantas dived steeply away
from the medusa, gaining speed by losing altitude.

Within minutes, they had vanished back into the wall of cloud from which they had emerged. And the medusa, no longer falling, began to roll back toward the horizontal. Soon it was sailing along once more on an even keel, as if nothing had happened.

"Beautiful!" said Dr. Brenner after a moment of stunned silence. "It's developed electric defenses—like some of our eels and rays. But that must have been about a million volts! Can you see any organs that might produce the discharge? Anything looking like electrodes?"

"No," Falcon answered, after switching to the highest power of the telescope. "But here's something odd. Do you see this pattern? Check back on the earlier images—I'm sure it wasn't there before."

A broad, mottled band had appeared along the side of the medusa. It formed a startlingly regular checkerboard, each square of which was itself speckled in a complex subpattern of short horizontal lines. They were spaced equal distances apart, in a geometrically perfect array of rows and columns.

"You're right," said Dr. Brenner, and now there was something very much like awe in his voice. "That's just appeared. And I'm afraid to tell you what I think it is."

"Well, I have no reputation to lose—at least as a biologist. Shall I give my guess?"

"Go ahead."

"That's a large meter-band radio array. The sort of thing they used back at the beginning of the twentieth century."

"I was afraid you'd say that. Now we know why it gave such a massive echo."

"But why has it just appeared?"

"Probably an aftereffect of the discharge."

"I've just had another thought," said Falcon rather slowly. "Do you suppose it's *listening* to us?"

"On this frequency? I doubt it. Those are meter— no, *decameter* antennas, judging by their size. Hmm . . . that's an idea!"

Dr. Brenner fell silent, obviously contemplating some new line of thought. Presently, he continued: "I bet they're tuned to the radio outbursts! That's something nature never got around to doing on Earth. We have animals with sonar and even electric senses, but nothing ever developed a radio sense. Why bother, where there was so much light?

"But it's different here. Jupiter is *drenched* with radio energy. It's worth while using it—maybe even tapping it. That thing could be a floating power plant!"

A new voice cut into the conversation.

"Mission Commander here. This is all very interesting—but there's a much more important matter to settle. *Is it intelligent?* If so, we've got to consider the First Contact directives."

"Until I came here," said Dr. Brenner somewhat ruefully, "I would have sworn that anything that can make a shortwave antenna system *must* be intelligent. Now I'm not sure. This could have evolved naturally. I suppose it's no more fantastic than the human eye."

"Then we have to play safe and assume intelligence. For the present, therefore, this expedition comes under all the clauses of the Prime Directive."

There was a long silence while everyone on the radio circuit absorbed the implications of this. For the first time in the history of space flight, the rules that had been established through more than a century of argument might have to be applied. Man had—it was hoped—profited from his mistakes on Earth. Not only moral considerations but his own self-interest demanded that he should not repeat them among the planets. It could be disastrous to treat a superior intelligence as the American settlers had treated the red Indians or as almost everyone had treated the Africans.

The first rule was: Keep your distance—make no attempt to approach nor even to communicate until "they" have had plenty of time to study you. Exactly what was meant by plenty of time no one had ever been able to decide; it was left to the discretion of the man on the spot.

A responsibility of which he had never dreamed had descended upon Howard Falcon. In the few hours that remained to him on Jupiter, he might become the first ambassador of the human race.

And *that* was an irony so delicious that he almost wished the surgeons had restored to him the power of laughter.

Prime Directive

IT WAS GROWING DARKER, BUT FALCON SCARCELY NOTICED as he strained his eyes toward that living cloud in the field of the telescope. The wind that was still sweeping *Kon-Tiki* steadily around the funnel of the great whirlpool had now brought him within twenty kilometers of the creature; if he got much closer than ten, he would take evasive action. Though he felt certain that the medusa's electric weapons were short-ranged, he did not wish to put the matter to the test. That would be a problem for future explorers, and he wished them luck.

Now it was quite dark in the capsule—and that was strange, because sunset was still hours away. Automatically, he glanced at the horizontally scanning radar, as he had done every few minutes. Apart from the medusa he was studying, there was no other object within a hundred kilometers of him.

Suddenly, with startling power, he heard the sound that had come booming out of the Jovian night—the throbbing beat that grew more and more rapid, then stopped mid-crescendo. The whole capsule vibrated with it, like a pea in a kettledrum.

Howard Falcon realized two things almost simultaneously, during the sudden, aching silence. *This* time, the sound was not coming from thousands of kilometers away, over a radio circuit. It was in the very atmosphere around him.

The second thought was even more disturbing. He had quite forgotten—it was inexcusable, but there had been other apparently more important things on his mind—that most of the sky above him was completely blanked out by *Kon-Tiki's* gasbag. Being lightly silvered to conserve its heat, the great balloon was an effective shield both to radar and to vision.

He had known this, of course; it had been a minor defect of the design, tolerated because it did not appear important. It seemed very important to Howard Falcon now—as he saw that fence of gigantic tentacles, thicker than the trunks of any tree, descending all around the capsule.

He heard Brenner yelling: "Remember the Prime Directive! Don't alarm it!" Before he could make an appropriate answer, that overwhelming drumbeat started again and drowned all other sounds.

The sign of a really skilled test pilot is how he reacts not to foreseeable emergencies but to ones that nobody could have anticipated. Falcon did not hesitate for more than a second to analyze the situation; then, in a lightning-swift movement, he pulled the rip cord.

That word was an archaic survival from the days of the first hydrogen balloons; on *Kon-Tiki*, the rip cord did not tear open the gasbag but merely operated a set of louvers round the upper curve of the envelope. At once, the hot gas started to rush out; *Kon-Tiki*, deprived of her lift, began to fall swiftly in this gravity field two and a half times as strong as Earth's.

Falcon had a momentary glimpse of great tentacles whipping upward and away; he had just time to note that they were studded with large bladders or sacs, presumably to give them buoyancy, and that they ended in multitudes of thin feelers like the roots of a plant. He half expected a bolt of lightning, but nothing happened.

His precipitous rate of descent was slackening as the atmosphere thickened and the deflated envelope acted as a parachute. *Kon-Tiki* had dropped more than three kilometers; it should be safe to close the louvers again. By the time he had restored buoyancy and was in equilibrium once more, he had lost another two kilometers of altitude and was getting dangerously near his safety limit.

He peered anxiously through the overhead windows, though he did not expect to see anything except the obscuring bulk of the balloon. But he had sideslipped during his descent and part of the medusa was just visible a couple of kilometers above him. It was much closer than he expected—and it was still coming down, faster than he would have believed possible.

Mission Control was calling anxiously; he shouted, "I'm OK—but it's still coming after me. I can't go any deeper."

That was not quite true. He could go a lot deeper—about 300 kilometers. But it would be a one-way trip and most of the journey would be of little interest to him.

Then, to his great relief, he saw that the medusa was leveling off about a kilometer above him. Perhaps it had decided to approach this strange intruder with caution—or perhaps it, too, found this deeper layer uncomfortably hot. The temperature was over fifty degrees and Falcon wondered how much longer his life-support system could handle matters.

Dr. Brenner was back on the circuit, still worrying about the Prime Directive.

"Remember—it may only be inquisitive!" he cried without much conviction. "Try not to frighten it!"

Falcon was getting rather tired of this advice and recalled a TV discussion he had once seen between a space lawyer and an astronaut. After the full implications of the Prime Directive had been carefully spelled out, the incredulous spacer had exclaimed: "So if there were no alternative, I must sit still and let myself be eaten?" The lawyer had not even cracked a smile when he answered: "That's an *excellent* summing up."

It had seemed funny at the time; it was not at all amusing now.

And then Falcon saw something that made him even more unhappy. The medusa was still hovering a kilometer above him—but one of its tentacles was becoming incredibly elongated and was stretching down toward *Kon-Tiki*, thinning out at the same time. As a boy, he had once seen the funnel of a tornado descending from a storm cloud over the Kansas plains; the thing coming toward him now evoked vivid memories of that black, twisting snake in the sky.

"I'm rapidly running out of options," he reported to Mission Control. "I now have only a choice between frightening it and giving it a bad stomach-ache. I don't think it will find *Kon-Tiki* very digestible, if that's what it has in mind."

He waited for comments from Brenner, but the biologist remained silent.

"Very well—it's twenty-seven minutes ahead of time, but I'm starting the ignition sequencer. I hope I'll have enough reserve to correct my orbit later."

He could no longer see the medusa; it was directly overhead once more. But he knew that the descending tentacle must now be very close to the balloon. It would take almost five minutes to bring the reactor up to full thrust.

The fusor was primed. The orbit computer had not rejected the situation as wholly impossible. The air scoops were open, ready to gulp in tons of the surrounding hydrohelium on demand. Even under optimum conditions, this would have been the moment of truth—for there had been no way of testing how a nuclear ram jet would *really* work in the strange atmosphere of Jupiter.

Very gently, something rocked *Kon-Tiki*. Falcon tried to ignore it.

Ignition had been planned ten kilometers higher than this, in an atmosphere of less than a quarter of the density—and 30 degrees cooler. Too bad.

What was the shallowest dive he could get away with for the air scoops to work? When the ram ignited, he'd be heading *toward* Jupiter, with two and a half *g* to help him get there. Could he possibly pull out in time?

A large, heavy hand patted the balloon. The whole vessel bobbed up and down, like one of the yo-yos that had just become the craze back on Earth.

Of course, Brenner *might* be perfectly right. Perhaps it was just trying to be friendly. Maybe he should try to talk to it over the radio. Which should it be: "Pretty pussy"? "Down, Fido!"? or "Take me to your leader"?

The tritium-deuterium ratio was correct. He was ready to light the candle, with a hundred-million-degree match.

The thin tip of the tentacle came slithering round the edge of the balloon, only twenty meters away. It was about the size of an elephant's trunk and by the delicate way it was moving, appeared to be almost as sensitive. There were little palps at its very end, like questing mouths. He was sure that Dr. Brenner would be fascinated.

This seemed about as good a time as any. He gave a swift scan of the entire control board, started the final four-second ignition count, broke the safety seal and pressed the JETTISON switch.

There was a sharp explosion and an instant loss of weight. *Kon-Tiki* was falling freely, nose down. Overhead, the discarded balloon was racing upward, dragging the inquisitive tentacle with it. Falcon had no time to see if the gasbag actually hit the medusa, because at that moment the ram jet fired and he had other matters to think about.

A roaring column of hot hydrohelium was pouring out of the reactor nozzles, swiftly building up thrust—but *toward* Jupiter, not away from it. He could not pull out yet, for vector control was too sluggish. Unless he could gain complete control and achieve horizontal flight within the next five seconds, the vehicle would dive too deeply into the atmosphere and would be destroyed.

With agonizing slowness—those five seconds seemed like fifty—he managed to flatten out, then pull the nose upward. He glanced back only once and caught a final glimpse of the medusa many kilometers away. _Kon-Tiki_'s discarded gasbag had apparently escaped from its grasp, for he could see no sign of it.

Now he was master once more—no longer drifting helplessly on the winds of Jupiter but riding his own column of atomic fire back to the stars. The ram jet would steadily give him velocity and altitude, until he had reached near orbital speed at the fringes of the atmosphere. Then, with a brief burst of pure rocket power, he would regain the freedom of space.

Halfway to orbit, he looked south and saw the tremendous enigma of the Great Red Spot—that floating island twice the size of Earth—coming up over the horizon. He stared into its mysterious beauty until the computer warned him that conversion to rocket thrust was only sixty seconds ahead, then tore his gaze reluctantly away.

"Some other time," he murmured.

"What's that?" said Mission Control. "What did you say?"

"It doesn't matter," he replied.

Between Two Worlds

"YOU'RE A HERO NOW, HOWARD," SAID WEBSTER, "NOT just a celebrity. You've given them something to think about—injected some excitement into their lives. Not one in a million will actually travel to the Outer Giants—but the whole human race will go in imagination. And that's what counts."

"I'm glad to have made your job a little easier."

Webster was too old a friend to take offense at the note of irony. Yet it surprised him; this was not the first change in Howard that he had noticed since the return from Jupiter.

The administrator pointed to the famous sign on his desk, borrowed from an impresario of an earlier age: ASTONISH ME!

"I'm not ashamed of my job. New knowledge, new resources—they're all very well. But men also need novelty and excitement. Space travel has become routine; you've made it a great adventure once more. It will be a long, long time before we get Jupiter pigeon-holed. And maybe longer still before we understand those medusae. I still think that one *knew* where your blind spot was. Anyway, have you decided on your next move? Saturn, Uranus, Neptune—you name it."

"I don't know. I've thought about Saturn, but I'm not really needed there. It's only one gravity, not two and a half like Jupiter. So men can handle it."

Men, thought Webster. He said men. He's never done that before. And when did I last hear him use the word we? He's changing—slipping away from us.

"Well," he said aloud, rising from his chair to conceal his slight uneasiness. "Let's get the conference started. The cameras are all set up and everyone's waiting. You'll meet a lot of old friends."

He stressed the last word, but Howard showed no response; the leathery mask of his face was becoming more and more difficult to read. Instead, he rolled back from the administrator's desk, unlocked his undercarriage so that it no longer formed a chair and rose on his hydraulics to his full seven feet of height. It had been good psychology on the part of the surgeons to give him that extra twelve inches as some compensation for all else that he had lost when the *Queen* had crashed.

He waited until Webster had opened the door, then pivoted neatly on his balloon tires and headed for it at a smooth and silent thirty kilometers an hour. The display of speed and precision was not flaunted arrogantly; already, it was quite unconscious.

Howard Falcon, who had once been a man and could still pass for one over a voice circuit, felt a calm sense of achievement—and, for the first time in years, something like peace of mind. Since his return from Jupiter, the nightmares had ceased. He had found his role at last.

He knew now why he had dreamed about that superchimp aboard the doomed *Queen Elizabeth*. Neither man nor beast, it was between two worlds; and so was he.

He alone could travel unprotected on the lunar surface; the life-support system inside the metal cylinder that had replaced his fragile body functioned equally well in space or under water. Gravity fields ten times that of Earth were an inconvenience but nothing more. And no gravity was best of all.

The human race was becoming more remote from him, the ties of kinship more tenuous. Perhaps these air-breathing, radiation-sensitive bundles of unstable carbon compounds had no right beyond the atmosphere; they should stick to their natural homes— Earth, Moon, Mars.

Some day, the real masters of space would be machines, not men—and he was neither. Already conscious of his destiny, he took somber pride in his unique loneliness—the first immortal, midway between two orders of creation.

He would, after all, be an ambassador; between the old and the new—between the creatures of carbon and the creatures of metal who must one day supersede them.

Both would have need of him in the troubled centuries that lay ahead.

THE BEST IN SCIENCE FICTION

Breath Rasps Over Knocking Heartbeats

Holes in the ice have been broken with ice axes; the rock below is good rock, lined with vertical fissures. A chunk of ice whizzes by, clatters on the face below.

Only the fixed rope makes it possible for Roger to ascend this pitch, it is so hard. Another chunk of ice flies by and both of them curse.

The sun disappears behind the cliff, leaving only the streetlamp light of the dusk mirrors. Arthur peers up at them as Marie stuffs their packs with the new rope. "Beautiful," he exclaims "They have parhelia on Earth, too, you know—a natural effect of the light when there's ice crystals in the atmosphere. It's usually seen in Antarctica—big haloes around the sun, and at two points of the halo these mock suns. But I don't think we ever had four mock suns per side. Beautiful!"

Also by Kim Stanley Robinson
published by Tor Books

The Memory of Whiteness
The Planet on the Table

KIM STANLEY ROBINSON

GREEN MARS

A TOM DOHERTY ASSOCIATES BOOK
NEW YORK

Reprinted by permission of the author and the author's agent, John Schaffner Associates.

GREEN MARS

A TOR Book
Published by Tom Doherty Associates, Inc.
49 West 24 Street
New York, NY 10010

ISBN: 0-812-53362-3   Can. ISBN: 0-812-55967-3

Library of Congress Catalog Card Number: 88-50473

First edition: October 1988

Printed in the United States of America

0 9 8 7 6 5 4 3 2 1

OLYMPUS MONS IS THE TALLEST MOUNTAIN IN THE SOLAR system. It is a broad shield volcano, six hundred kilometers in diameter and twenty-seven kilometers high. Its average slope angles only five degrees above the horizontal, but the circumference of the lava shield is a nearly continuous escarpment, a roughly circular cliff that drops six kilometers to the surrounding forests. The tallest and steepest sections of this encircling escarpment stand near South Buttress, a massive prominence which juts out and divides the south and south-east curves of the cliff (on the map, it's at 15 degrees North, 132 degrees West). There, under the east flank of South Buttress, one can stand in the rocky upper edge of the Tharsis forest, and look up at a cliff that is twenty-two thousand feet tall.

* * *

Seven times taller than El Capitan, three times as tall as Everest's southwest face, twice as tall as Dhaulagiri wall: four miles of cliff, blocking out the western sky. Can you imagine it? (It's hard.)

"I can't get a sense of the scale!" the Terran, Arthur Sternbach, shouts, hopping up and down.

Dougal Burke, looking up through binoculars, says, "There's quite a bit of foreshortening from here."

"No, no. That's not it."

The climbing party has arrived in a caravan of seven field-cars. Big green bodies, clear bubbles covering the passenger compartments, fat field tires with their exaggerated treads, chewing dust into the wind: the cars' drivers have parked the cars in a rough circle, and they sit in the middle of a rocky meadow like a big necklace of paste emeralds.

This battered meadow, with its little stands of bristlecone pine and noctis juniper, is the traditional base camp for South Buttress climbs. Around the cars are treadmarks, wind-walls made of stacked rock, half-filled latrine trenches, cairn-covered trash dumps, and discarded equipment. As the members of the expedition wander around the camp, stretching and talking, they inspect some of these artifacts. Marie Whillans picks up two Ultralite oxygen cylinders stamped with letters that identify them as part of an expedition she climbed with more than a century ago. Grinning, she holds them overhead and shakes them at the cliff, beats them together. "Home again!" *Ping! Ping! Ping!*

* * *

One last field-car trundles into the meadow, and the expedition members already in the camp gather around it as it rolls to a halt. Two men get out of the car. They are greeted enthusiastically: "Stephan's here! Roger's here!"

But Roger Clayborne is in a bad mood. It has been a long trip for him. It began in Burroughs six days ago, when he left his offices at the Government House for the last time. Twenty-seven years of work as Minister of the Interior came to an end as he walked out the tall doors of Government House, down the broad marble steps and onto the trolley that would take him to his flat. Riding along with his face in the warm wind, Roger looked out at the tree-filled capital city he had rarely left during his stint in the government, and it struck him that it had been twenty-seven years of continuous defeat. Too many opponents, too many compromises, until the last unacceptable compromise arrived, and he found himself riding out of the city with Stephan, into the countryside he had avoided for twenty-seven years, over rolling hills covered by grasses and studded by stands of walnut, aspen, oak, maple, eucalyptus, pine: every leaf and every blade of grass a sign of his defeat. And Stephan wasn't much help; though a conservationist like Roger, he had been a member of the Greens for years. "That's where the real work can be done," he insisted as he lectured Roger and neglected his driving. Roger, who liked Stephan well enough, pretended his agreement and stared out his window. He would have preferred Stephan's company in smaller doses—say a lunch, or a game of batball. But on they drove along the wide gravel highway, over the windblown steppes of the

Tharsis bulge, past the farms and towns in Noctis
Labyrinthus, down into the forests of east Tharsis,
until Roger fell prey to that feeling one gets near the
end of a long journey, that all his life had been part of
this trip, that the traveling would never end this side
of the grave, that he was doomed to wander over the
scenes of all his defeats and failures endlessly, and
never come to any place that did not include them all,
right in the rearview mirror. It was a long drive.

For—and this was the worst of it—he remembered
everything.

Now he steps from the car door to the rocky soil of
base camp. A late addition to the climb (Stephan
invited him along when he learned of the resignation),
he is introduced to the other climbers, and he musters
the cordial persona built over many years in office.
"Hans!" he says as he sees the familiar smiling face of
the areologist Hans Boethe. "Good to see you. I didn't
know you were a climber."

"Not one like you, Roger, but I've done my share in
Marineris."

"So"—Roger gestures west—"are you going to find
the explanation for the escarpment?"

"I already know it," Hans declares, and the others
laugh. "But if we find any contributing evidence . . ."

A tall rangy woman with leathery cheeks and light
brown eyes appears at the edge of the group. Stephan
quickly introduces her. "Roger, this is our expedition
leader, Eileen Monday."

"We've met before," she says quickly as she shakes
his hand. She looks down and smiles an embarrassed

smile. "A long time ago, when you were a canyon guide."

The name, the voice; the past stirs, quick images appear in his mind's eye, and Roger's uncanny memory calls back a hike—(he once guided treks through the fossae canyon to the north)—a *romance*, yes, with a leggy girl: Eileen Monday, standing now before him. They were lovers for quite some time, he recalls; she a student in Burroughs, a city girl, and he—off in the back country. It hadn't lasted. But that was over two hundred years ago! A spark of hope strikes in him— "You *remember*?" he says.

"I'm afraid not." Wrinkles fan away under her eyes as she squints, smiles the embarrassed smile. "But when Stephan told me you'd be joining us—well— you're known to have a complete memory, and I felt I should check. Maybe that means I did remember something. Because I went through my old journals and found references to you. I only started writing the journals in my eighties, so the references aren't very clear. But I know we met, even if I can't say I remember it." She looks up, shrugs.

It is a common enough situation for Roger. His "total recall" (it is nothing of the sort, of course) encompasses most of his three hundred years, and he is constantly meeting and remembering people who do not recall him. Most find it interesting, some unnerving; this Eileen's sun-chapped cheeks are a bit flushed; she seems both embarrassed and perhaps a bit amused. "You'll have to tell me about it," she says with a laugh.

Roger isn't in the mood to amuse people. "We were about twenty-five."

Her mouth forms a whistle. "You really do remember everything."

Roger shakes his head; the chill in the shadowed air fills him, the momentary thrill of recognition and recall dissipates. It's been a very long trip.

"And we were . . .?" she prods.

"We were friends," Roger says, with just the twist on _friends_ to leave her wondering. It is disheartening, this tendency of people to forget; his unusual facility makes him a bit of a freak, a voice from another time. Perhaps his conservation efforts grow out of this retention of the past; he still knows what the planet was like, back there in the beginning. When he's feeling low he tends to blame his generation's forgetfulness on their lack of vigilance, and he is often, as he is now, a bit lonely.

Eileen has her head crooked, wondering what he means.

"Come on, Mr. Memory," Stephan cries to him. "Let's eat! I'm starving, and it's freezing out here."

"It'll get colder," Roger says. He shrugs at Eileen, follows Stephan.

In the bright lamplight of the largest base camp tent the chattering faces gleam. Roger sips at a bowl of hot stew. Quickly the remaining introductions are made. Stephan, Hans, and Eileen are familiar to him, as is Dr. Frances Fitzhugh. The lead climbers are Dougal Burke and Marie Whillans, current stars of New Scotland's climbing school; he's heard of both of them. They are surrounded in their corner by four younger colleagues of Eileen's, climbing guides hired by Stephan to be their porters: "We're the Sherpas," Ivan Vivanov says to Roger cheerfully, and introduces

Ginger, Sheila, and Hannah. The young guides appear not to mind their supporting role in the expedition; in a party of this size there will be plenty of climbing for all. The group is rounded off by Arthur Sternbach, an American climber visiting Hans Boethe. When the introductions are done they all circle the room like people at any cocktail party anywhere. Roger works on his stew and regrets his decision to join the climb. He forgot (sort of) how intensely social big climbs must be. Too many years of solo bouldering, in the rock valleys north of Burroughs. That was what he had been looking for, he realizes: an endless solo rockclimb, up and out of the world.

Stephan asks Eileen about the climb and she carefully includes Roger in her audience. "We're going to start up the Great Gully, which is the standard route for the first thousand meters of the face. Then, where the first ascent followed the Nansen Ridge up to the left of the gully, we're planning to go right. Dougal and Marie have seen a line in the aerial photos that they think will go, and that will give us something new to try. So we'll have a new route most of the way. And we'll be the smallest party ever to climb the scarp in the South Buttress area."

"You're kidding!" Arthur Sternbach cries.

Eileen smiles briefly. "Because of the party size, we'll be carrying as little oxygen as possible, for use in the last few thousand meters."

"And if we climb it?" Roger asks.

"There's a cache for us when we top out—we'll change equipment there, and stroll on up to the caldera rim. That part will be easy."

"I don't see why we even bother with that part," Marie interjects.

"It's the easiest way down. Besides, some of us want to see the top of Olympus Mons," Eileen replies mildly.

"It's just a big hill," says Marie.

Later Roger leaves the tent with Arthur and Hans, Dougal and Marie. Everyone will spend one last night of comfort in the cars. Roger trails the others, staring up at the escarpment. The sky above it is still a rich twilight purple. The huge bulk of the wall is scarred by the black line of the Great Gully, a deep vertical crack just visible in the gloomy air. Above it, a blank face. Trees rustle in the wind; the dark meadow looks wild.

"I can't believe how tall it is!" Arthur is exclaiming for the third time. He laughs out loud. "It's just unbelievable!"

"From this vantage," Hans says, "the top is over seventy degrees above our real horizon."

"You're kidding! I can't believe it!" And Arthur falls into a fit of helpless giggling. The Martians following Hans and his friend watch with amused reserve. Arthur is quite a bit shorter than the rest of them, and suddenly to Roger he seems like a child caught after breaking into the liquor cabinet. Roger pauses to allow the others to walk on.

The big tent glows like a dim lamp, luminous yellow in the dark. The cliff-face is black and still. From the forest comes a weird yipping yodel. Some sort of mutant wolves, no doubt. Roger shakes his head. Long ago any landscape exhilarated him; he was in love with the planet. Now the immense cliff seems to hang over him like his life, his past, obliterating the sky, blocking off any progress westward. The depression he feels is so crushing that he almost sits on the meadow grass, to plunge his face in his hands; but others will be leaving the tent. Again, that mournful yowling: the planet, crying out, Mars is gone! Mars is gone! Owoooooooooo! Homeless, the old man goes to sleep in a car.

But as always, insomnia takes its share of the night. Roger lies in the narrow bed, his body relaxed, his consciousness bouncing helplessly through scenes from his life. Insomnia, memory: some of his doctors have told him there is a correlation between the two. Certainly for him the hours of insomniac awareness and half-sleep are memory's playground, and no matter what he does to fill the time between lying down and falling asleep (like reading to exhaustion, or scratching notes), tyrannical memory will have its hour.

This night he remembers all the nights in Burroughs. All the opponents, all the compromises. The Chairman handing him the order to dam and flood Coprates Chasma, with his little smile and flourish, the touch of hidden sadism. The open dislike from Noyova, that evening years before, after the Chairman's appointments: "The Reds are finished, Clayborne. You shouldn't be holding office—you are the leader of a dead party." Looking at the Chairman's dam construction bill and thinking of Coprates the way it had been in the previous century, when he had explored it, it occurred to him that ninety percent of what he had done in office, he did to stay in a position to be able to do anything. That was what it meant to work in government. Or was it a higher percentage? What had he really done to preserve the planet? Certain bills balked before they began, certain development projects delayed; all he had done was resist the doings of others. Without much success. And it could even be said that walking out on the Chairman and his "coalition" cabinet was only another gesture, another defeat.

He recalls his first day in office. A morning on the polar plains. A day in Burroughs, in the park. In the Cabinet office, arguing with Novoyov. And on it will go, for another hour or more, scene after scene until the memories become fragmented and dreamlike, spliced together surrealistically, stepping outside the realm of memory into sleep.

There are topographies of the spirit, and this is one of them.

Dawn on Mars. First the plum sky, punctuated by a diamond pattern of four dawn mirrors that orbit overhead and direct a little more of Sol's light to the planet. Flocks of black choughs caw sleepily as they flap and glide out over the talus slope to begin the day's hunt for food. Snow pigeons coo in the branches of a grove of tawny birch. Up in the talus, a clatter of rocks; three Dall sheep are looking surprised to see the base camp meadow occupied. Sparrows flit overhead.

Roger, up early with a headache, observes all the stirring wildlife indifferently. He hikes up into the broken rock of the talus to get clear of it. The upper rim of the escarpment is struck by the light of the rising sun, and now there is a strip of ruddy gold overhead, bathing all the shadowed slope below with reflected sunlight. The dawn mirrors look dim in the clear violet sky. Colors appear in the tufts of flowers scattered through the rock, and the green juniper needles glow. The band of lit cliff quickly grows; even in full light the upper slopes look sheer and blank. But that is the effect of distance and foreshortening. Lower on the face, crack systems look like brown rain stains, and the wall is rough-looking, a good sign. The upper slopes, when they get high enough, will reveal their own irregularities.

Dougal hikes out of the rock field, ending some dawn trek of his own. He nods to Roger. "Not started yet, are we?" His English is accented with a distinctly Scottish intonation.

In fact they are. Eileen and Marie and Ivan have gotten the first packs out of the cars, and when Roger and Dougal return they are distributing them. The meadow becomes noisier as the long equipment sorting ends and they get ready to take off. The packs are heavy, and the Sherpas groan and joke when they lift theirs. Arthur can't help laughing at the sight of them. "On Earth you couldn't even *move* a pack that size," he exclaims, nudging one of the oversized bags with a foot. "How do you balance with one of these on?"

"You'll find out," Hans tells him cheerfully.

Arthur finds that balancing the mass of his pack in Martian gravity is difficult. The pack is almost perfectly cylindrical, a big green tube that extends from the bottom of his butt to just over his head; with it on his back he looks like a tall green snail. He exclaims at its lightness relative to its size, but as they hike through the talus its mass swings him around much more than he is prepared for. "Whoah! Look out there! Sorry!" Roger nods and wipes sweat from his eye. He sees that the first day is one long lesson in balance for Arthur, as they wind their way up the

irregular slope through the forest of house-sized boulders.

Previous parties have left a trail with rock ducks
and blazes chopped onto boulder faces, and they
follow it wherever they can find it. The ascent is
tedious; although this is one of the smaller fans of
broken rock at the bottom of the escarpment (in some
areas mass wasting has collapsed the entire cliff into
talus), it will still take them all of a very long day to
wind their way through the giant rockpile to the
bottom of the wall proper, some seven hundred
meters above base camp.

At first Roger approves of the hike through the
jumbled field of house-sized boulders. "The Khumbu
Rockfall," Ivan calls out, getting into his Sherpa
persona as they pass under a big stone serrac. But
unlike the Khumbu Icefall below the fabled Everest,
this chaotic terrain is relatively stable; the overhangs
won't fall on them, and there are few hidden crevasses
to fall into. No, it is just a rockfield, and Roger likes it.
Still, on the way they pass little pockets of chir pine
and juniper, and ahead of Roger, Hans apparently
feels obliged to identify every flower to Arthur.
"There's aconite, and those are anemones, and that's
a kind of iris, and those are gentians, and those are
primulas. . . ." Arthur stops to point. "What the hell
is that!"

Staring down at them from a flat-topped boulder is
a small furry mammal. "It's a dune dog," Hans says
proudly. "They've clipped some marmot and Weddell
seal genes onto what is basically a wolverine."

"You're kidding! It looks like a miniature polar
bear."

Behind them Roger shakes his head, kicks idly at a stand of tundra cactus. It is flowering; the six-month Martian spring is beginning. Syrtis grass tufting in every wet sandy flat. Little biology experiments, everywhere you look; the whole planet one big laboratory. Roger sighs. Arthur tries to pick one of each variety of flower, making a bouquet suitable for a state funeral, but after too many falls he gives up, and lets the colorful bundle hang from his hand. Late in the day they reach the bottom of the wall. The whole world is in shadow, while the clear sky overhead is still a bright lavender. Looking up they cannot see the top of the escarpment any more; they will not see it again unless their climb succeeds.

Camp One is a broad, flat circle of sand, surrounded by boulders that were once part of the face, and set under a slight overhang formed by the sheer rampart of basalt that stands to the right side of the Great Gully. Protected from rockfall, roomy and comfortable to lie on, Camp One is perfect for a big lower camp, and it has been used before; between the rocks they find pitons, oxygen cylinders, buried latrines overgrown with bright green moss.

The next day they wind their way back down through the talus to Base Camp—all but Dougal and Marie, who take the day to look at the routes leading out of Camp One. For the rest of them, it's off before dawn, and down through the talus at nearly a running pace; a quick reloading; and back up in a race to reach Camp One again before nightfall. Every one of the next four days will be spent in the same way, and the Sherpas will continue for three more days after that,

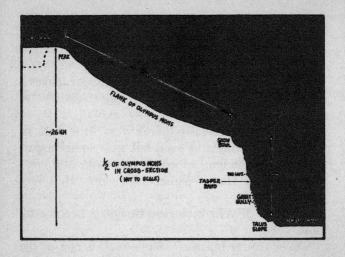

threading the same trail through the boulders, until all
the equipment has been lugged up to Camp One.

In the same way that a tongue will go to a sore tooth
over and over, Roger finds himself following Hans
and Arthur to hear the areologist's explanations. He
has realized, to his chagrin, that he is nearly as
ignorant about what lives on Mars as Arthur is.

"See the blood pheasant?"

"No."

"Over there. The head tuft is black. Pretty well
camouflaged."

"You're kidding. Why, there it is!"

"They like these rocks. Blood pheasants, redstarts,
accentors—more of them here than we ever see."

Later: "Look there!"

"Where?"

Roger finds himself peering in the direction Hans has pointed.

"On the tall rock, see? The killer rabbit, they call it. A joke."

"Oh, a joke," Arthur says carefully. Roger makes a revision in his estimation of the Terran's subtlety. "A rabbit with fangs?"

"Not exactly. Actually there's very little hare in it—more lemming and pika, but with some important traits of the lynx added. A very successful creature. Some of Harry Whitebook's work. He's *very* good."

"So some of your biological designers become famous?"

"Oh yes. Very much so. Whitebook is one of the best of the mammal designers. And we seem to have a special love for mammals, don't we?"

"I know I do." Several puffing steps up waist-high blocks. "I just don't understand how they can survive the cold!"

"Well, it's not that cold down here, of course. This is the top of the alpine zone, in effect. The adaptations for cold are usually taken directly from arctic and antarctic creatures. Many seals can cut the circulation to their extremeties when necessary to preserve heat. And they have a sort of anti-freeze in their blood—a glycoprotein that binds to the surface of ice crystals and stops their growth—stops the accumulation of salts. Wonderful stuff. Some of these mammals can freeze limbs and thaw them without damage to the flesh."

"You're kidding," Roger whispers as he hikes. "You're kidding!"

"And these adaptations are part of most Martian mammals. Look! There's a little foxbear! That's Whitebook again."

Roger stops following them. No more Mars.

Black night. The six big box tents of Camp One glow like a string of lamps at the foot of the cliff. Roger, out in the rubble relieving himself, looks back at them curiously. It is, he thinks, an odd group. People from all over Mars (and a Terran). Only climbing in common. The lead climbers are funny. Dougal sometimes seems a mute, always watching from a corner, never speaking. A self-enclosed system. Maria speaks for both of them, perhaps. Roger can hear her broad Midlands voice now, hoarse with drink, telling someone how to climb the face. She's happy to be here. Roger? He shakes his head, returns to the tents.

Inside Eileen's tent he finds a heated discussion in progress. Marie Whillans says, "Look, Dougal and I have already gone nearly a thousand meters up these so-called blank slabs. There are cracks all over the place."

"As far as you've gone there are," Eileen says. "But the true slabs are supposed to be above those first cracks. Four hundred meters of smooth rock. We could be stopped outright."

"So we could, but there's got to be _some_ cracks. And we can bolt our way up any really blank sections if we have to. That way we'd have a completely new route."

Hans Boethe shakes his head. "Putting bolts in some of this basalt won't be any fun."

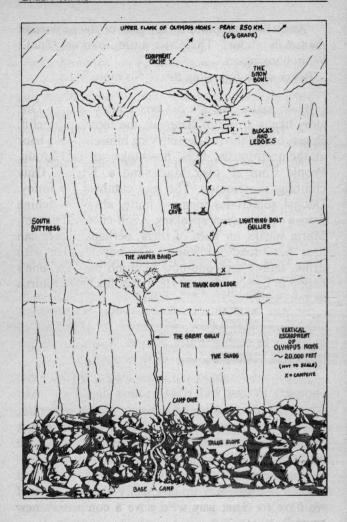

we time to." That way we'd save a considerable new
route."

Hans Boethe shakes his head. "Putting bolts in
some of this fresh won't be any fun."

"I hate bolts anyway," Eileen says. "The point is, if we take the Gully up to the first amphitheater, we know we've got a good route to the top, and all the upper pitches will be new."

Stephan nods, Hans nods, Frances nods. Roger sips a cup of tea and watches with interest. Marie says, "The *point* is, what kind of climb do we want to have?"

"We want to get to the top," Eileen says, glancing at Stephan, who nods. Stephan has paid for most of this expedition, and so in a sense it's his choice.

"Wait a second," Marie says sharply, eyeing each of them in turn. "That's not what it's about. We're not here just to repeat the Gully route, are we?" Her voice is accusing and no one meets her eye. "That wasn't what I was told, anyway. I was told we were taking a new route, and that's why I'm here."

"It will inevitably be a new route," Eileen says. "You know that, Marie. We trend right at the top of the Gully and we're on new ground. We only avoid the blank slabs that flank the Gully to the right!"

"I think we should try those slabs," Marie says, "because Dougal and I have found they'll go." She argues for this route, and Eileen listens patiently. Stephan looks worried; Marie is persuasive, and it seems possible that her forceful personality will overwhelm Eileen's, leading them onto a route rumored to be impossible.

But Eileen says, "Climbing *any* route on this wall with only eleven people will be doing something. Look, we're only talking about the first 1200 meters of the climb. Above that we'll tend to the right whenever possible, and be on new ground above these slabs."

"I don't believe in the slabs," Marie says. And after a few more exchanges: "Well, that being the case, I don't see why you sent Dougal and me up the slabs these last few days."

"I didn't send you up," Eileen says, a bit exasperated. "You two choose the leads, you know that. But this is a fundamental choice, and I think the Gully is the opening pitch we came to make. We do want to make the top, you know. Not just of the wall, but the whole mountain."

After more discussion Marie shrugs. "Okay. You're the boss. But it makes me wonder. Why are we making this climb?"

On the way to his tent Roger remembers the question. Breathing the cold air, he looks around. In Camp One the world seems a place creased and folded: horizontal half stretching away into darkness—back down into the dead past; vertical half stretching up to the stars—into the unknown. Only two tents lit from within now, two soft blobs of yellow in the gloom. Roger stops outside his darkened tent to look at them, feeling they say something to him; the eyes of the mountains, looking. . . . Why is he making this climb?

Up the Great Gully they go. Dougal and Marie lead pitch after pitch up the rough, unstable rock, hammering in pitons and leaving fixed ropes behind. The ropes tend to stay in close to the right wall of the gully, to avoid the falling rocks that shoot down it all too frequently. The other climbers follow from pitch to pitch in teams of two and three. As they ascend they can see the four Sherpas, tiny animals winding their way down the talus again.

Roger has been teamed with Hans for the day. They clip themselves onto the fixed rope with jumars, metal clasps that will slide up the rope but not down. They are carrying heavy packs up to Camp 2, and even though the slope of the Gully is only fifty degrees here, and its dark rock knobby and easy to climb, they both find the work hard. The sun is hot and their faces are quickly bathed with sweat.

"I'm not in the best of shape for this," Hans puffs. "It may take me a few days to get my rhythm."

"Don't worry about me," Roger says. "We're going about as fast as I like."

"I wonder how far above Camp 2 is?"

"Not too far. Too many carries to make, without the power reels."

"I look forward to the vertical pitches. If we're going to climb we might as well climb, eh?"

"Especially since the power reels will pull our stuff up."

"Yes." Breathless laugh.

Steep, deep ravine. Medium gray andesite, an igneous volcanic rock, speckled with crystals of dark minerals, knobbed with hard protrusions. Pitons hammered into small vertical cracks.

Midday they meet with Eileen, Arthur, and Frances, the team above, who are sitting on a narrow ledge in the wall of the Gully, jamming down a quick lunch. The sun is nearly overhead; in an hour they will lose it. Roger and Hans are happy to sit on the ledge. Lunch is lemonade and several handfuls of the trail

mix Frances has made. The others discuss the gully
and the day's climb, and Roger eats and listens. He
becomes aware of Eileen sitting on the ledge beside
him. Her feet kick the wall casually, and the quadri-
ceps on the tops of her thighs, big exaggerated muscles, bunch and relax, bunch and relax, stretching the
fabric of her climbing pants. She is following Hans's
description of the rock and appears not to notice
Roger's discreet observation. Could she really *not
remember* him? Roger breathes a soundless sigh. It's
been a long life. And all his effort—

"Let's get up to Camp 2," Eileen says, looking at
him curiously.

Early in the afternoon they find Marie and Dougal
on a broad shelf sticking out of the steep slabs to the
right of the Great Gully. Here they make Camp 2: four
large box tents, made to withstand rockfalls of some
severity.

Now the verticality of the escarpment becomes
something immediate and tangible. They can only see
the wall for a few hundred meters above them; beyond
that it is hidden, except up the steep trough in the wall
that is the Great Gully, etching the vertical face just
next to their shelf. Looking up this giant couloir they
can see more of the endless cliff above them, dark and
foreboding against the pink sky.

Roger spends an hour of the cold afternoon sitting
at the Gully edge of their shelf, looking up. They have
a long way to go; his hands in their thick pile mittens
are sore, his shoulders and legs tired, his feet cold. He
wishes more than anything that he could shake the

depression that fills him; but thinking that only makes it worse.

Eileen Monday sits beside him. "So we were friends once, you say."

"Yeah." Roger looks her in the eye. "You don't remember at all?"

"It was a long time ago."

"Yes. I was twenty-six, you were about twenty-three."

"You really remember that long ago?"

"Some of it, yes."

Eileen shakes her head. She has good features, Roger thinks. Fine eyes. "I wish I did. But as I get older my memory gets even worse. Now I think for every year I live I lose at least that much in memories. It's sad. My whole life before I was seventy or eighty —all gone." She sighs. "I know most people are like that, though. You're an exception."

"Some things seem to be stuck in my mind for good," says Roger. He can't believe it isn't true of everyone! But that's what they all say. It makes him melancholy. Why live at all? What's the point? "Have you hit your three hundredth yet?"

"In a few months. But—come on. Tell me about it."

"Well . . . you were a student. Or just finishing school, I can't remember." She smiles. "Anyway, I was guiding groups in hikes through the little canyons north of here, and you were part of a group. We started up a—a little affair, as I recall. And saw each other for a while after we got back. But you were in Burroughs, and I kept guiding tours, and—well, you know. It didn't last."

Eileen smiles again. "So I went on to become a mountain guide—which I've been for as long as I can remember—while you moved to the city and got into politics!" She laughs and Roger smiles wryly. "Obviously we must have impressed each other!"

"Oh yes, yes." Roger laughs shortly. "Searching for each other." He grins lopsidedly, feeling bitter. "Actually, I only got into government about forty years ago. Too late, as it turned out."

Silence for a while. "So that's what's got you down," Eileen says.

"What?"

"The Red Mars party—out of favor."

"Out of existence, you mean."

She considers it. "I never could understand the Red point of view—"

"Few could, apparently."

"—Until I read something in Heidegger, where he makes a distinction between *earth* and *world*. Do you know it?"

"No."

"*Earth* is that blank materiality of nature that exists before us and more or less sets the parameters on what we can do. Sartre called it facticity. *World* then is the human realm, the social and historical dimension that gives earth its meaning."

Roger nods his understanding.

"So—the Reds, as I understood it, were defending earth. Or planet, in this case. Trying to protect the primacy of planet over world—or at least to hold a balance between them."

"Yes," Roger said. "But the world inundated the planet."

"True. But when you look at it that way, you can see what you were trying to do was hopeless. A political party is inevitably part of the world, and everything it does will be wordly. And we only know the materiality of nature through our human senses—so really it is only world that we know directly."

"I'm not sure about that," Roger protested. "I mean, it's logical, and usually I'm sure it's true—but sometimes"—He smacks the rock of their shelf with his mittened hand. "You know?"

Eileen touches the mitten. "World."

Roger lifts his lip, irritated. He pulls the mitten off and hits the cold rock again. "Planet."

Eileen frowns thoughtfully. "Maybe."

And there *was* hope, Roger thought fiercely. We could have lived on the planet the way we found it, and confronted the materiality of earth every day of our lives. We could have.

Eileen is called away to help with the arrangement of the next day's loads. "We'll continue this later," she says, touching Roger lightly on the shoulder.

He is left alone over the Gully. Moss discolors the stone under him, and grows in cracks in the couloir. Swallows shoot down the Gully like falling stones, hunting for cliff mice or warm-blooded lizards. To the east, beyond the great shadow of the volcano, dark forests mark the sunlit Tharsis bulge like blobs of lichen. Nowhere can one see Mars, just Mars, the primal Mars. Clenching a cold, rope-sore fist, Roger thinks, *They forgot.* They forgot what it was like to walk out onto the empty face of old Mars.

Once he walked out onto the Great Northern Desert. All of Mars's geographical features are immense by Terran scales, and just as the southern hemisphere is marked by huge canyons, basins, volcanoes, and craters, the northern hemisphere is strangely, hugely smooth; in fact it had, in its highest latitudes, surrounding what at that time was the polar ice cap (it is now a small sea), a planet-ringing expanse of empty, layered sand. Endless desert. And one morning before dawn Roger walked out of his campsite and hiked a few kilometers over the broad wave-like humps of the windswept sand, and sat down on the crest of one of the highest waves. There was no sound but his breath, his blood pounding in his ears, and the slight hiss of the oxygen regulator in his helmet. Light leaked over the horizon to the southeast and began to bring out the sand's dull ochre, flecked with dark red. When the sun cracked the horizon the light bounced off the short steep faces of the dunes and filled everything. He breathed the gold air, and something in him bloomed, he became a flower in a garden of rock, the sole consciousness of the desert, its focus, its soul. Nothing he had ever felt before came close to matching this exaltation, this awareness of brilliant light, of illimitable expanse, of the glossy, intense *presence* of material things. He returned to his camp late in the day, feeling that a moment had passed—or an age. He was nineteen years old, and his life was changed.

Just being able to remember that incident, after two hundred and eighty-odd years have passed, makes Roger a freak. Less than one percent of the population share this gift (or curse) of powerful, long-term recollection. These days Roger feels the ability like a weight—as if each year were a stone, so that now he carries the crushing burden of three hundred red stones everywhere he goes. He feels angry that others forget. Perhaps it is envious anger.

Thinking of that walk when he was nineteen reminds Roger of a time years later, when he read Herman Melville's novel _Moby Dick_. The little black cabin boy Pip (and Roger had always identified himself with Pip in _Great Expectations)_, "the most insignificant of the _Pequod's_ crew," fell overboard while his whaleboat was being pulled by a harpooned whale. The boat flew onward, leaving Pip alone. "The intense concentration of self in the middle of such a heartless immensity, my God! who can tell it?" Abandoned on the ocean surface alone, Pip grew more and more terrified, until "By the merest chance the ship itself at last rescued him; but from that hour the little Negro went about the deck an idiot. . . . The sea had jeeringly kept his finite body up, but drowned the infinite of his soul."

Reading that made Roger feel strange. Someone had lived an hour very like his day on the polar desert, out in the infinite void of nature. And what had seemed to Roger rapture, had driven Pip insane.

It occurred to him, as he stared at the thick book, that perhaps he had gone mad as well. Terror, rapture —these extremities of emotion circumnavigate the spirit and approach each other again, though departing from the origin of perception in opposite directions. Mad with solitude, ecstatic with Being—the two parts of the recognition of self sit oddly together. But Pip's insanity only shocked Roger into a sharper love for his own experience of the "heartless immensity." He *wanted* it; and suddenly all the farthest, most desolate reaches of Mars became his special joy. He woke at night and sat up to watch dawns, the flower in the garden of rock. And wandered days like John in the desert, seeing God in stones and frost and skies that arched like sheets of fire.

Now he sits on a ledge on a cliff on a planet no longer his, looking down on plains and canyons peppered with life, life *created by the human mind*. It is as if the mind has extruded itself into the landscape: each flower an idea, each lizard a thought. . . . There is no heartless immensity left, no mirror of the void for the self to see itself in. Only the self, everywhere, in everything, suffocating the planet, cloying all sensation, imprisoning every being.

Perhaps this perception itself was a sort of madness.

The sky itself, after all (he thought), provides a heartless immensity beyond the imagination's ability to comprehend, night after night.

Perhaps he needed an immensity he could imagine the extent of, to feel the perception of it as ecstasy rather than terror.

Roger sits remembering his life and thinking over these matters, as he tosses granules of rock—little pips—over the ledge into space.

To his surprise, Eileen rejoins him. She sits on her heels, recites quietly,

> *"I love all waste*
> *And solitary places, where we taste*

> *The pleasures of believing what we see*
> *Is boundless, as we wish our souls to be."*

"Who said that?" Roger asks, startled by the lines.

"Shelley," Eileen replies. "In 'Julian and Maddalo.'"

"I like it."

"Me too." She tosses a pip over herself. "Come join us for dinner?"

"What? Oh, sure, sure. I didn't know it was time."

That night, the sound of the tent scraping stone, as the wind shifts it and shifts it. The scritching of thought as world scrapes against planet.

Next day they start spreading out. Marie, Dougal, Hannah, and Ginger take off early up the Gully, around a rib and out of sight, leaving behind a trail of fixed rope. Occasionally those left below can hear their voices, or the ringing of a piton being hammered into the hard rock. Another party descends to Camp 1, to begin dismantling it. When they have got everything up to Camp 2, the last group up will bring the fixed ropes up with them. Thus they will set rope above them and pull it out below them, all the way up the wall.

Late the next day Roger climbs up to carry more rope to Marie and Dougal and Hannah and Ginger. Frances comes with him.

The Great Gully is steeper above Camp 2, and after a few hours of slow progress Roger finds his pack growing very heavy. His hands hurt, the foot-holds grow smaller and smaller, and he finds he must stop after every five or ten steps. "I just don't have it today," he says as Frances takes over the lead.

"Me neither," she says, wheezing for air. "I think we'll have to start using oxygen during the climbing pretty soon."

But the lead climbers do not agree. Dougal is working his way up a constriction in the Gully, knocking ice out of a crack with his ice axe, then using his fists for chocks and his twisted shoe soles for a staircase, and stepping up the crack as fast as he can clear it. Marie is belaying him and it is left to Hannah and Ginger to greet Roger and Frances. "Great, we were just about to run out of rope."

Dougal stops and Marie takes the opportunity to point to the left wall of the Gully. "Look," she says, disgusted. Roger and Frances see a streak of light blue—a length of xylar climbing rope, hanging free from a rust-pitted piton. "That Terran expedition, I bet," Marie says. "They left ropes the entire way, I hear."

From above Dougal laughs.

Marie shakes her head. "I hate seeing stuff like that."

Frances says, "I think we'd better go onto oxygen pretty soon."

She gets some surprised stares. "Why?" asks Marie. "We've barely started."

"Well, we're at about four kilometers above the datum—"

"Exactly," Marie says. "I *live* higher than that."

"Yes, but we're working pretty hard here, and going up pretty fast. I don't want anyone to get edema."

"I don't feel a thing," Marie says, and Hannah and Ginger nod.

"I could use a bit of oxygen," Dougal says from above, grinning down at them briefly.

"You don't feel edema till you have it," Frances says stiffly.

"Edema," says Marie, as if she doesn't believe in it.

"Marie's immune," Dougal calls down. "Her head can't get more swollen than it already is."

Hannah and Ginger giggle at Marie's mock glare, her tug on the rope to Dougal.

"Down you come, boy."

"On your head."

"We'll see how the weather goes," Frances says. "But either way, if we make normal progress we'll be needing oxygen soon."

This is apparently too obvious to require comment. Dougal reaches the top of the crack, and hammers in a piton; the ringing strikes grow higher and higher in pitch as the piton sets home.

That afternoon Roger helps the leads set up a small wall tent. The wall tents are very narrow and have a stiff inflatable floor; they can be hung from three pitons if necessary, so that the inhabitants rest on an air-filled cushion hanging in space, like window-washers. But more often they are placed on ledges or indentations in the cliff-face, to give the floor some support. Today they have found that above the narrowing of the Great Gully is a flattish indentation protected by an overhang. The cracks above the indentation are poor, but with the addition of a couple of rock bolts the climbers look satisfied. They will be protected from rockfall, and tomorrow they can venture up to find a better spot for Camp 3 without delay. As there is just barely room (and food) for two, Roger and Frances begin the descent to Camp 2.

During the descent Roger imagines the cliff face as flat ground, entertained by the new perspective this gives. Ravines cut into that flat land: vertically these are called gullies, or couloirs, or chimneys, depending on their shape and tilt. Climbing in these gives the climber an easier slope and more protection. Flat land has hills, and ranges of hills: these vertically are knobs, or ridges, or shelfs, or buttresses. Depending on their shape and tilt these can either be obstacles, or in the case of some ridges, easy routes up. Then walls become ledges, and creeks become cracks—although cracking takes its own path of least resistance, and seldom resembles water-carved paths.

As Roger belays Frances down one difficult pitch (they can see more clearly why their climb up was so tiring), he looks around at what little he can see: the gray and black walls of the gully, some distance above and below him; the steep wall of the rampart to the left of the gully. And that's all. A curious duality; because this topography stands near the vertical, in many ways he will never see it as well as he would an everyday horizontal hillside. But in other ways (looking right into the grain of the rock to see if one nearly detached knob will hold the weight of his entire body for a long step down, for instance) he sees it much more clearly, more *intensely* than he will ever ever see the safe world of flatness. This intensity of vision is something the climber treasures.

The next day Roger and Eileen team up, and as they ascend the gully with another load of rope, a rock the

size of a large person falls next to them, chattering
over an outcropping and knocking smaller rocks
down after it. Roger stops to watch it disappear below.
The helmets they are wearing would have been no
protection against a rock that size.

"Let's hope no one is following us up," Roger says.

"Not supposed to be."

"I guess getting out of this gully won't be such a bad
idea, eh?"

"Rockfall is almost as bad on the face. Last year
Marie had a party on the face when a rock fell on a
traverse rope and cut it. Client making the traverse
was killed."

"A cheerful business."

"Rockfall is bad. I hate it."

Surprising emotion in her voice; perhaps some
accident had occurred under her leadership as well?
Roger looks at her curiously. Odd to be a climbing
guide and not be more stoic about such dangers.

Then again, rockfall is the danger beyond expertise.
She looks up: distress. "You know."

He nods. "No precautions to take."

"Exactly. Well, there are some. But they aren't
really sufficient."

The lead climbers' camp is gone without a trace,
and a new rope leads up the left wall of the gully,
through a groove in the overhang and out of sight
above. They stop to eat and drink, then continue up.
The difficulty of the next pitch impresses them; even
with the rope it is hard going. They wedge into the
moat between a column of ice and the left wall, and
inch up painfully. "I wonder how long this lasts,"
Roger says, wishing they had their crampons with

them. Above him, Eileen doesn't reply for over a
minute. Then she says, "Three hundred more meters," as if out of the blue. Roger groans theatrically,
client to guide.

Actually he is enjoying following Eileen up the
difficult pitch. She has a quick rhythm of observation
and movement that reminds him of Dougal, but her
choice of holds is all her own—and closer to what
Roger would choose. Her calm tone as they discuss the
belays, her smooth pulls up the rock, the fine propor-
tions of her long legs, reaching for the awkward
foothold: a beautiful climber. And every once in a
while there is a little jog at Roger's memory.

Three hundred meters above they find the lead
climbers, out of the gully and on a flat ledge that
covers nearly a hectare, on the left side this time.
From this vantage they can see parts of the cliff face to
the right of the gully, above them. "Nice campsite,"
Eileen remarks. Marie, Dougal, Hannah, and Ginger
are sitting about, resting in the middle of setting up
their little wall tents. "Looked like you had a hard day
of it down there."

"Invigorating," Dougal says, eyebrows raised.

Eileen surveys them. "Looks like a little oxygen
might be in order." The lead group protests. "I know,
I know. Just a little. A cocktail."

"It only makes you crave it," Marie says.

"Maybe so. We can't use much down here, anyway."

In the midday radio call to the camps below, Eileen
tells the others to pack up the tents from Camp 1.
"Bring those and the power reels up first. We should
be able to use the reels between these camps."

They all give a small cheer. The sun disappears behind the cliff above, and they all groan. The leads stir themselves and continue setting up the tents. The air chills quickly.

Roger and Eileen descend through the afternoon shadows to Camp 2, as there is not enough equipment to accommodate more than the lead group at Camp 3. Descending is easy on the muscles compared to the ascent, but it requires just as much concentration as going up. By the time they reach Camp 2 Roger is very tired, and the cold sunless face has left him depressed again. Up and down, up and down.

That night during the sunset radio conversation Eileen and Marie get into an argument when Eileen orders the leads down to do some portering. "Look, Marie, the rest of us haven't led a single pitch, have we? And we didn't come on this climb to ferry up goods for you, did we?" Eileen's voice has a very sharp, cutting edge to it when she is annoyed. Marie insists the first team is making good time, and is not tired yet. "That's not the point. Get back down to Camp 1 tomorrow, and finish bringing it up. The bottom team will move up and reel Camp 2 up to 3, and those of us here at 2 will carry one load up to 3 and have a bash at the lead after that. That's the way it is, Marie—we leapfrog in my climbs, you know that."

Sounds behind the static from the radio, of Dougal talking to Marie. Finally Marie says, "Aye, well you'll need us more when the climbing gets harder anyway. But we can't afford to slow down much."

After the radio call Roger leaves the tent and sits on his ledge bench to watch the twilight. Far to the east the land is still sunlit, but as he watches the landscape darkens, turns dim purple under the blackberry sky. Mirror dusk. A few stars sprinkle the high dome above him. The air is cold but still, and he can hear Hans and Frances inside their tent, arguing about glacial polish. Frances is an areologist of some note, and apparently she disagrees with Hans about the origins of the escarpment; she spends some of her climbing time looking for evidence in the rock.

Eileen sits down beside him. "Mind?"

"No," he says.

She says nothing, and it occurs to him she may be upset. He says, "I'm sorry Marie is being so hard to get along with."

She waves a mittened hand to dismiss it. "Marie is always like that. It doesn't mean anything. She just wants to climb." She laughs. "We go on like this every time we climb together, but I still like her."

"Hmph." Roger raises his eyebrows. "I wouldn't have guessed."

She does not reply. For a long time they sit there. Roger's thoughts return to the past, and helplessly his spirits plummet again.

"You seem . . . disturbed about something," Eileen ventures.

"Ehh," Roger says. "About everything, I suppose." And winces to be making such a confessional. But she appears to understand; she says,

"So you fought all the terraforming?"

"Most of it, yeah. First as head of a lobbying group. You must be part of it now—Martian Wilderness Explorers."

"I pay the dues."

"Then in the Red government. And in the Interior

Ministry, after the Greens took over. But none of it
did any good."

"And why, again?"

"*Because*," he bursts out—stops—starts again:
"Because I liked the planet the way it was when we
found it! A lot of us did, back then. It was so
beautiful . . . or not just that. It was more overwhelming than beautiful. The size of things, their shapes—
the whole planet had been evolving, the landforms
themselves, I mean, for five billion years, and traces of
all that time were still on the surface to be seen and
read, if you knew how to look. It was so wonderful to
be out there. . . ."

"The sublime isn't always beautiful."

"True. It transcended beauty, it really did. One time
I walked out onto the polar desert, you know. . . ."
But he doesn't know how to tell it. "And so, and so it
seemed to me that we already had an Earth, you
know? That we didn't need a Terra up here. And
everything they did eroded the planet that we came to.
They destroyed it! And now we've got—whatever.
Some kind of park. A laboratory to test out new plants
and animals and all. And everything I loved so much
about those early years is gone. You can't find it
anywhere anymore."

In the dark he can just see her nodding. "And so
your life's work . . ."

"Wasted!" He can't keep the frustration out of his
voice. Suddenly he doesn't want to, he wants her to
understand what he feels, he looks at her in the dark,
"A three-hundred year life, entirely wasted! I mean I
might as well have just . . ." He doesn't know what.

Long pause.

"At least you can remember it," she says quietly.

"What good is that? I'd rather forget, I tell you."

"Ah. You don't know what that's like."

"Oh, the past. The God-damned past. It isn't so great. Just a dead thing."

She shakes her head. "Our past is never dead. Do you know Sartre's work?"

"No."

"A shame. He can be a big help to we who live so long. For instance, in several places he suggests that there are two ways of looking at the past. You can think of it as something dead and fixed forever; it's part of you, but you can't change it, and you can't change what it means. In that case your past limits or even controls what you can be. But Sartre doesn't agree with that way of looking at it. He says that the past is constantly altered by what we do in the present moment. The *meaning* of the past is as fluid as our freedom in the present, because every new act that we commit can revalue the entire thing!"

Roger humphs. "Existentialism."

"Well, whatever you want to call it. It's part of Sartre's philosophy of freedom, for sure. He says that the only way we can possess our past—whether we can remember it or not, I say—is to add new acts to it, which then give it a new value. He calls this 'assuming' our past."

"But sometimes that may not be possible."

"Not for Sartre. The past is always assumed, because we are *not* free to stop creating new values for it. It's just a question of what those values will be. For Sartre it's a question of *how* you will assume your past, not whether you will."

"And for you?"

"I'm with him on that. That's why I've been reading

him these last several years. It helps me to understand things."

"Hmph." He thinks about it. "You were an English major in college, did you know that?"

But she ignores the comment. "So—" She nudges him lightly, shoulder to shoulder. "You have to decide how you will assume this past of yours. Now that Mars is gone."

He considers it.

She stands. "I have to plunge into the logistics for tomorrow."

"Okay. See you inside."

A bit disconcerted, he watches her leave. Dark tall shape against the sky. The woman he remembers was not like this. In the context of what she has just said, the thought almost makes him laugh.

For the next few days all the members of the team are hard at work ferrying equipment up to Camp 3, except for two a day who are sent above to find a route to the next camp. It turns out there is a feasible reeling route directly up the gully, and most of the gear is reeled up to Camp 3 once it is carried to Camp 2. Every evening there is a radio conversation, in which Eileen takes stock and juggles the logistics of the climb, and gives the next day's orders. From other camps Roger listens to her voice over the radio, interested in the relaxed tone, the method she has of making her decisions right in front of them all, and the easy way she shifts her manner to accommodate whoever she is speaking with. He decides she is very good at her job, and wonders if their conversations are simply a part of that. Somehow he thinks not.

*   *   *

Roger and Stephan are given the lead, and early one
mirror dawn they hurry up the fixed ropes above
Camp 3, turning on their helmet lamps to aid the
mirrors. Roger feels strong in the early going. At the
top of the pitch the fixed ropes are attached to a nest
of pitons in a large, crumbling crack. The sun rises
and suddenly bright light glares onto the face. Roger
ropes up, confirms the signals for the belay, starts up
the gully.

The lead at last. Now there is no fixed rope above
him determining his way; only the broad flat back and
rough walls of the gully, looking much more vertical
than they have up to this point. Roger chooses the
right wall and steps up onto a rounded knob. The wall
is a crumbling, knobby andesite surface, black and a
reddish gray in the harsh morning blast of light; the
back wall of the gully is smoother, layered like a very
thick-grained slate, and broken occasionally by horizontal cracks. Where the back wall meets the side wall
the cracks widen a bit, sometimes offering perfect
footholds. Using them and the many knobs of the wall
Roger is able to make his way upward. He pauses
several meters above Stephan at a good-looking vertical crack to hammer in a piton. Getting a piton off the
belt sling is awkward. When it is hammered in he pulls
a rope through and jerks on it. It seems solid. He
climbs above it. Now his feet are spread, one in a
crack, one on a knob, as his fingers test the rock in a
crack above his head; then up, and his feet are both on
a knob in the intersection of the walls, his left hand far
out on the back wall of the gully to hold on to a little
indention. Breath rasps in his throat. His fingers get
tired and cold. The gully widens out and grows
shallower, and the intersection of back and side walls

becomes a steep narrow ramp of its own. Fourth piton in, the ringing hammer strikes filling the morning air. New problems: the degraded rock of this ramp offers no good cracks, and Roger has to do a tension traverse over to the middle of the gully to find a better way up. Now if he falls he will swing back into the side wall like a pendulum. And he's in the rockfall zone. Over to the left side wall, quickly a piton in. Problem solved. He loves the immediacy of problem solving in climbing, though at this moment he is not aware of his pleasure. Quick look down: Stephan a good distance away, and below him! Back to concentrating on the task at hand. A good ledge, wide as his boot, offers a resting place. He stands, catches his breath. A tug on the line from Stephan; he has run out of rope. Good lead, he thinks, looking down the steep gully at the trail left by the green rope, looping from piton to piton. Perhaps a better way to cross the gully from right to left? Stephan's helmeted face calls something up. Roger hammers in three pitons and secures the line. "Come on up!" he cries. His fingers and calves are tired. There is just room to sit on his bootledge: immense world, out there under the bright pink morning sky! He sucks down the air and belays Stephan's ascent, pulling up the rope and looping it carefully. The next pitch will be Stephan's; Roger will have quite a bit of time to sit on this ledge and feel the intense solitude of his position in this vertical desolation. "Ah!" he says. Climbing up and out of the world. . . .

It is the strongest sort of duality: facing the rock and climbing, his attention is tightly focused on the rock within a meter or two of his eyes, inspecting its every flaw and irregularity. It is not particularly good climbing rock, but the gully slopes at about seventy degrees in this section, so the actual technical difficulty is not that great. The important thing is to *understand* the rock fully enough to find only good holds and good cracks—to recognize suspect holds and avoid them. A lot of weight will follow them up these fixed ropes, and although the ropes will probably be renailed, his piton placement will likely stand. One has to see the rock and the world beneath the rock.

And then he finds a ledge to sit and rest on, and turns around, and there is the great rising expanse of the Tharsis Bulge. Tharsis is a continent-sized bulge in the Martian surface; at its center it is eleven kilometers above the Martian datum, and three prince volcanoes lie in a line, northeast to southwest on the bulge's highest plateau. Olympus Mons is at the far northwestern edge of the bulge, almost on the great expanse of Amazonis Planitia. Now, not even half way up the great volcano's escarpment, Roger can just see the three prince volcanoes poking over the horizon to the southeast, demonstrating perfectly the size of the planet itself. He looks around one-eighteenth of Mars.

By midafternoon Roger and Stephan have run out of their 300 meters of rope, and they return to Camp 3 pleased with themselves. The next morning they hurry up the fixed ropes in the mirror dawn, and begin again. At the end of Roger's third pitch in the lead he comes upon a good site for a camp: a sort of pillar bordering the Great Gully on its right side ends abruptly in a flat top that looks very promising. After negotiating a difficult short traverse to get onto the pillar top, they wait for the midday radio conference.

Consultation with Eileen confirms that the pillar is about the right distance from Camp 3, and suddenly they are standing in Camp 4.

"The Gully ends pretty near to you anyway," Eileen says.

So Roger and Stephan have the day free to set up a wall tent and then explore. The climb is going well, Roger thinks: no major technical difficulties, a group that gets along fairly well together . . . perhaps the great South Buttress will not prove to be that difficult after all.

Stephan gets out a little sketchbook. Roger glances at the filled pages as Stephan flips through them. "What's that?"

"Chir pine, they call it. I saw some growing out of the rocks above Camp 1. It's amazing what you find living on the side of this cliff!"

"Yes," Roger says.

"Oh, I know, I know. You don't like it. But I'm sure I don't know why." He has a blank sheet of the sketchbook up now. "Look in the cracks across the gully. Lot of ice there, and then patches of moss. That's moss campion, with the lavender flowers on top of the moss cushion, see?"

He begins sketching and Roger watches, fascinated. "That's a wonderful talent to have, drawing."

"Skill. Look, there's edelweiss and asters, growing almost together." He jerks, puts finger to lips, points. "Pika," he whispers.

Roger looks at the broken niches in the moat of the gully opposite them. There is a movement and suddenly he sees them—two little gray furballs with bright black eyes—three—the last scampering up the rock fearlessly. They have a hole at the back of one

niche for a home. Stephan sketches rapidly, getting
the outline of the three creatures, then filling them in.
Bright Martian eyes.

And once, in the Martian autumn in Burroughs,
when the leaves covered the ground and fell through
the air, leaves the color of sand, or the tan of ante-
lopes, or the green of green apples, or the white of
cream, or the yellow of butter—he walked through
the park. The wind blew stiffly from the southwest out
of the big funnel of the delta, bringing clouds flying
overhead swiftly, scattered and white and sunbroken
to the west, bunched up and dark dusky blue to the
east; and the evergreens waved their arms in every
shade of dark green, before which the turning leaves of
the hardwoods flared; and above the trees to the east a
white-walled church, with reddish arched roof tiles
and a white bell tower, glowed under the dark clouds.
Kids playing on the swings across the park, yellow-red
aspens waving over the brick city hall beyond them to
the north—and Roger felt—wandering among
widely-spaced white-trunked trees that thrust their
white limbs in every upward direction—he felt—
feeling the wind loft the gliding leaves over him—he
felt what all the others must have felt when they
walked around, that Mars had become a place of
exquisite beauty. In such lit air he could see every
branch, leaf and needle waving under the tide of wind,
crows flying home, lower clouds lofting puffy and
white under the taller black ones, and it all struck him
all at once: freshly colored, fully lit, spacious and alive
in the wind—what a world! What a world.
   And then, back in his offices, he hadn't been able to
tell anyone about it. It wouldn't have been like him.

Remembering that, and remembering his recent talk with Eileen, Roger feels uncomfortable. His past overpowered that day's walk through the park: what kind of assumption was that?

Roger spends his afternoon free climbing above Camp 4, looking around a bit and enjoying the exercise of his climbing skills. They're coming back very quickly. But the rock is nearly crack-free once out of the Gully, and he decides free climbing is not a good idea. Besides, he's noticed a curious thing: about fifty meters above Camp 4, the Great Central Gully is gone. It ends in a set of overhangs like the ribs under the protruding wall of a building. Definitely not the way up. And yet the face to the right of the overhangs is not much better; it too tilts out and out, until it is almost sheer. The few cracks breaking this mass will not be easy to climb. In fact, Roger doubts he *could* climb them, and wonders if the leads are up to it. Well, sure, he thinks, they can climb anything. But it looks awful. Hans has talked about the volcano's "hard eon," when the lava pouring from the caldera was denser and more consistent than in the volcano's earlier years. The escarpment, being a sort of giant boring of the volcano's flow history, naturally reflects the changes in lava consistency in its many horizontal bands. So far they have been climbing on softer rock—now they have reached the bottom of a harder band. Back in Camp 4 Roger looks up at what he can see of the cliff above and wonders where they will go.

Another duality: the two halves of the day, forenoon and afternoon. Forenoon is sunny and therefore hot: a morning ice and rock shower in the Gully, and time to dry out sleeping bags and socks. Then noon passes and the sun disappears behind the cliff above. For an hour or so they have the weird half-light of the dusk mirrors, then they too disappear, and suddenly the air is biting, bare hands risk frostnip, and the lighting is indirect and eerie: a world in shadow. Water on the cliff-face ices up, and rocks are pushed out—there is another period when rocks fall and go whizzing by. People bless their helmets and hunch their shoulders in, and discuss again the possibility of shoulder pads. In the cold the cheery morning is forgotten, and it seems the whole climb takes place in shadow.

When Camp 4 is established, they try several reconnaissance climbs through what Hans calls the Jasper Band. "It looks like orbicular jasper, see?" He shows them a dull rock and after cutting away at it with a laser saw shows them a smooth brown surface, speckled with little circles of yellow, green, red, white. "Looks like lichen," Roger says. "Fossilized lichen."

"Yes. This is orbicular jasper. For it to be trapped in this basalt implies a metamorphic slush—lava partially melting rock in the throat above the magma chamber, and then throwing it all up. . . ."

So it was the Jasper Band, and it was trouble. Too sheer—close to vertical, really, and without an obvious way up. "At least it's good hard rock," Dougal says cheerfully.

Then one day Arthur and Marie return from a long traverse out to the right, and then up. They hurry into camp grinning ear to ear.

"It's a ledge," Arthur says. "A perfect ledge. I can't believe it. It's about half a meter wide, and extends around this rampart for a couple hundred meters, just like a damn sidewalk! We just walked right around that corner! Completely vertical above and below—talk about a view!"

For once Roger finds Arthur's enthusiasm fully appropriate. The Thank God Ledge, as Arthur has named it ("There's one like this in Yosemite"), is a horizontal break in the cliff-face, and a flat slab just wide enough to walk on is the result. Roger stops in the middle of the ledge to look around. Straight up: rock and sky. Straight down: the tiny tumble of the talus, appearing directly below them, as Roger is not inclined to lean out too far to see the rock in between. The exposure is astonishing. "You and Marie walked along this ledge without ropes?" Roger says.

"Oh, it's fairly wide," Arthur replies. "Don't you think? I ended up crawling there where it narrows just a bit. But mostly it was fine. Marie walked the whole way."

"I'm sure she did." Roger shakes his head, happy to be clipped onto the rope that has been fixed about chest high above the ledge. With its aid he can appreciate this strange ledge—perfect sidewalk in a completely vertical world: the wall hard, knobby, right next to his head—under him the smooth surface of the ledge, and then empty space.

Verticality. Consider it. A balcony high on a tall building will give a meager analogy: experience it. On the side of this cliff, unlike the side of any building, there is no ground below. The world below is the world of belowness, the rush of air under your feet.

The forbidding smooth wall of the cliff, black and upright beside you, halves the sky. Earth, air; the solid here and now, the airy infinite; the wall of basalt, the sea of gases. Another duality: to climb is to live on the most symbolic plane of existence and the most physical plane of existence *at the same time.* This too the climber treasures.

At the far end of the Thank God Ledge there is a crack system that breaks through the Jasper Band—it is like a narrow, miniature version of the Great Gully, filled with ice. Progress upward is renewed, and the cracks lead up to the base of an ice-filled half-funnel, that divides the Jasper Band even further. The bottom of the funnel is sloped just enough for Camp 5, which becomes by far the most cramped of the campsites. The Thank God Ledge traverse means that using the power reels is impossible between Camps 4 and 5, however. Everyone makes ten or twelve carries between the two camps. Each time Roger walks the sidewalk through space, his amazement at it returns.

While the carries across the ledge are being made, and Camps 2 and 3 are being dismantled, Arthur and Marie have begun finding the route above. Roger goes up with Hans to supply them with rope and oxygen. The climbing is "mixed," half on rock, half on black ice rimmed with dirty hard snow. Awkward stuff. There are some pitches that make Roger and Hans gasp with effort, look at each other round-eyed. "Must have been Marie leading." "I don't know, that Arthur is pretty damn good." The rock is covered in many places by layers of black ice, hard and brittle—years

of summer rain followed by frost have caked the
exposed surfaces at this height. Roger's boots slip over
the slick ice repeatedly. "Need crampons up here."

"Except the ice is so thin, you'd be kicking rock."

"Mixed climbing."

"Fun, eh?"

Breath rasps over knocking heartbeats. Holes in the
ice have been broken with ice-axes; the rock below is
good rock, lined with vertical fissures. A chunk of ice
whizzes by, clatters on the face below.

"I wonder if that's Arthur and Marie's work."

Only the fixed rope makes it possible for Roger to
ascend this pitch, it is so hard. Another chunk of ice
flies by, and both of them curse.

Feet appear in the top of the open-book crack they
are ascending.

"Hey! Watch out up there! You're dropping ice
chunks on us!"

"Oh! Sorry, didn't know you were there." Arthur
and Marie jumar down the rope to them. "Sorry,"
Marie says again. "Didn't know you'd come up so
late. Have you got more rope?"

"Yeah."

The sun disappears behind the cliff, leaving only the
streetlamp light of the dusk mirrors. Arthur peers up
at them as Marie stuffs their packs with the new rope.
"Beautiful," he exclaims. "They have parhelia on
Earth, too, you know—a natural effect of the light
when there's ice crystals in the atmosphere. It's usually seen in Antarctica—big haloes around the sun, and
at two points of the halo these mock suns. But I don't
think we ever had four mock suns per side. Beautiful!"

"Let's go," Marie says without looking up. "We'll
see you two down at Camp 5 tonight." And off they

go, using the rope and both sides of the open-book crack to quickly lever their way up.

"Strange pair," Stephan says as they descend to Camp 5.

The next day they take more rope up. In the late afternoon, after a very long climb, they find Arthur and Marie, sitting in a cave in the side of the cliff that is big enough to hold their entire base camp. "Can you believe this?" Arthur cries. "It's a damn hotel!"

The cave's entrance is a horizontal break in the cliff face, about four meters high and over fifteen from side to side. The floor of the cave is relatively flat, covered near the entrance with a thin sheet of ice, and littered with chunks of the roof, which is bumpy but solid. Roger picks up one of the rocks from the floor and moves it to the side of the cave, where floor and roof come together to form a narrow crack. Marie is trying to get somebody below on the radio, to tell them about the find. Roger goes to the back of the cave, some twenty meters in from the face, and ducks down to inspect the jumble of rocks in the long crack where floor and roof meet. "It's going to be nice to lay out flat for once," Stephan says. Looking out the cave's mouth Roger sees a wide smile of lavender sky.

When Hans arrives he gets very excited. He bangs about in the gloom hitting things with his ice axe, pointing his flashlight into various nooks and crannies. "It's tuff, do you see?" he says, holding up a chunk for their inspection. "This is a shield volcano, meaning it ejected very little ash over the years, which is what gave it its flattened shape. But there must have been a few ash eruptions, and when the ash is compressed it becomes tuff—this rock here. Tuff is much softer than basalt and andesite, and over the years this exposed layer has eroded away, leaving us with our wonderful hotel."

"I love it," says Arthur.

The rest of the team joins them in the mirror dusk, but the cave is still uncrowded. Although they set up tents to sleep in, they place the lamps on the cave floor, and eat dinner in a large circle, around a collection of glowing little stoves. Eyes gleam with laughter as the climbers consume bowls of stew. There is something marvelous about this secure home, tucked in the face of the escarpment three thousand meters above the plain. It is an unexpected joy to loll about on flat ground, unharnessed. Hans has not stopped prowling the cave with his flashlight. Occasionally he whistles.

"Hans!" Arthur calls when the meal is over and the bowls and pots have been scraped clean. "Get over here, Hans. Have a seat. There you go. Sit down." Marie is passing around her flask of brandy. "All right, Hans, tell me something. Why is this cave here? And why, for that matter, is this escarpment here? Why is Olympus Mons the only volcano anywhere to have this encircling cliff?"

Frances says, "It's not the *only* volcano to have such a feature."

"Now, Frances," Hans says. "You know it's the only big shield volcano with a surrounding escarpment. The analogies from Iceland that you're referring to are just little vents of larger volcanoes."

Frances nods. "That's true. But the analogy may still hold."

"Perhaps." Hans explains to Arthur: "You see,

there is still not a perfect agreement as to the cause of the scarp. But I think I can say that my theory is generally accepted—wouldn't you agree, Frances?"

"Yes . . ."

Hans smiles genially, and looks around at the group. "You see, Frances is one of those who believe that the volcano originally grew up through a glacial cap, and that the glacier made in effect a retaining wall, holding in the lava and creating this drop-off after the glacial cap disappeared."

"There are good analogies in Iceland for this particular shape for a volcano," Frances says. "And it's eruption under and through ice that explains it."

"Be that as it may," Hans says, "I am among those who feel that the *weight* of Olympus Mons is the cause of the scarp."

"You mentioned that once before," Arthur says, "but I don't understand how that would work."

Stephan voices his agreement with this, and Hans sips from the flask with a happy look. He says,

"The volcano is extremely old, you understand. Three or four billion years, on this same site, or close to it—very little tectonic drift, unlike on Earth. So, magma upwells, lava spills out, over and over and over, and it is deposited over softer material— probably the gardened regolith that resulted from the intensive meteor bombardments of the planet's earliest years. A tremendous weight is deposited on the surface of the planet, you see, and this weight increases as the volcano grows. As we all know now, it is a very, very big volcano. And eventually the weight is so great that it squishes out the softer material beneath it. We find this material to the northeast, which is the downhill side of the Tharsis bulge, and is naturally the side that the pressured rock would be pushed out to. Have any of you visited the Olympus Mons aureole?" Several of the climbers nod. "Fascinating region."

"Okay," Arthur says, "but why wouldn't that just sink the whole area? I would think that there would be a depression circling the edge of the volcano, rather than this cliff."

"Exactly!" Stephan cries.

But Hans is shaking his head, a smile on his face. He gestures for the brandy flask again. "The point is, the lava shield of Olympus Mons is a single unit of rock—layered, admittedly, but essentially one big cap of basalt, placed on a slightly soft surface. Now by far the greatest part of the weight of this cap is near the center—the volcano's peak, you know, still so far above us. So—the cap is a unit, a single piece of rock—and basalt has a certain flexibility to it, as all rock does. So the cap itself is somewhat flexible. Now the center of the cap sinks the farthest, being heaviest —and the outside edge of the shield, being part of a single flexible cap, _bends upward._"

"Up twenty thousand feet?" Arthur demands, incredulous. "You're kidding!"

Hans shrugs. "You must remember that the volcano stands twenty-five kilometers above the surrounding plains. The volume of the volcano is one hundred times the volume of Earth's largest volcano, Mauna Loa, and for three billion years at least it has been pressing down on this spot."

"But it doesn't make sense that the scarp would be so symmetrical if that was what happened," Frances objected.

"On the contrary. In fact that is the really wonderful aspect of it. The outer edge of the lava shield is lifted up, okay? Higher and higher, until the flexibility of the basalt is *exceeded*. In other words, the shield is just so flexible and no more. At the point where the stress becomes too much, the rock sheers off, and the inner side of the break continues to rise, while what is beyond the break point subsides. So, the plains down below us are still part of the lava aureole of Olympus Mons, but they are beyond the break point. And as the lava was everywhere approximately the same thickness, it gave way everywhere at about the same distance from the peak, giving us the roughly circular escarpment, which we now climb!"

Hans waves a hand with an architect's pride. Frances sniffs. Arthur says, "It's hard to believe." He taps the floor. "So the other half of this cave is underneath the talus wash down there?"

"Exactly!" Hans beams. "Though the other half was never a cave. This was probably a small, roughly circular layer of tuff, trapped in much harder basaltic lava. But when the shield broke and the escarpment was formed, the tuff deposit was cut in half, exposing its side to erosion. And a few eons later we have our cozy cave."

"Hard to believe," Arthur says again.

Roger sips from the flask and silently agrees with Arthur. It's remarkable how difficult it is to transfer the areologist's theories, in which mountains act like plastic or toothpaste, to the vast hard basalt reality underneath and above them. "It's the amount of time necessary for these transformations that's difficult to imagine," he says aloud. "It must take . . ." he waves a hand.

"Billions of years," Hans says. "We cannot properly

imagine that amount of time. But we can see the sure
signs of its passing."

And in three centuries we can destroy those signs,
Roger says silently. Or most of them. And make a park
instead.

Above the cave the cliff face lays back a bit, and the
smoothness of the Jasper Band is replaced by a
jumbled, complicated slope of ice gullies, buttresses,
and shallow horizontal slits that mimic their cave
below. These steps, as they call them, are to be
avoided like crevasses on level ground, as the over-
hanging roof of each is a serious obstacle. The ice
gullies provide the best routes up, and it becomes a
matter of navigating up what appears to be a vertical
delta, like the tracing of a lightning bolt burned into
the face and then frozen. Every morning as the sun
hits the face there is an hour or so of severe ice and
rock fall, and in the afternoons in the hour after the
sun leaves there is another period of rockfall. There
are some close calls and one morning Hannah is hit by
a chunk of ice in the chest, bruising her badly. "This
trick is to stay in the moat between the ice in the gully
and the rock wall," Marie says to Roger as they retreat
down a dead-end couloir.

"Or to be where you want to be by the time the sun
comes up," Dougal adds. And on his advice to Eileen,
they begin rising before dawn to make the exposed
parts of the climb. In the frigid dark a wristwatch
alarm beeps. Roger twists in his bag, trying to turn it
off; but it is his tent mate's. With a groan he sits up,
reaches over and switches on his stove. Soon the metal
rings in the top of the cubical stove are glowing a
friendly warm orange, heating the tent's air and giving

a little bit of light to see by. Eileen and Stephan are sitting in their bags, beating sleep away. Their hair is tousled, their faces lined, puffy, tired. It is three A.M. Eileen puts a pot of ice on the stove, dimming their light. She turns on a lamp to its lowest illumination, which is still enough to make Stephan groan. Roger digs in a food pouch for tea and dried milk. Breakfast is wonderfully warming, but suddenly he has to visit the cave's convenient yet cold latrine. Boots on—the worst part of dressing. Like sticking one's feet into iceblocks. Then out of the warm tent into the intense cold of the cave's air. Through the dark to the latrine. The other tents glow dimly; time for another dawn assault on the upper slopes.

By the time Archimedes, the first dawn mirror, appears, they have been on the slopes above the cave for nearly an hour, climbing by the light of their helmet lamps. The mirror dawn is better; there is enough light to see well, and yet the rock and ice have not been warmed enough to start falls. Roger climbs the ice gullies using crampons; he enjoys using them, kicking into the plastic ice with the front points of the crampons, and adhering to the slopes as if glued to them. Below him Arthur keeps singing a song in tribute to crampons: "Spiderman, Spiderman, Spiderman, Spidermannnnn . . ." But once above the fixed ropes, there is no extra breath for singing; the lead climbing is extremely difficult. Roger finds himself spread-eagled on one pitch, right foot spiked into the icefall, left foot digging into a niche the size of his toenail; left hand holding the shaft of the ice axe, which is firmly planted in the icefall above, and right hand laboriously turning the handle of an ice screw, which will serve as piton in this little couloir: and for a moment he realizes he is ten meters above the nearest belay, *hanging there by three tiny points.* And gasping for breath.

At the top of that pitch there is a small outcropping to rest on, and when Eileen pulls herself up the fixed rope she finds Roger and Arthur laid out over the rock in the morning sunlight like fish set out to dry. She surveys them as she catches her wind, gasping herself. "Time for oxygen," she declares. In the midday radio call she tells the next teams up to bring oxygen bottles along with the tents and other equipment for the next camp.

With three camps established above the cave, which serves as a sort of base camp to return to from time to time, they are making fair progress. Each night only a few of them are in any given camp. They are forced to use oxygen for almost all of the climbing, and most of them sleep with a mask on, the regulator turned to its lowest setting. The work of setting up the high camps, which they try to do without oxygen, becomes exhausting and cold. When the camps are set and the day's climbing is done, they spend the shadowed afternoons wheezing around the camps, drinking hot fluids and stamping their feet to keep them warm, waiting for the sunset radio call and the next day's orders. At this point it's a pleasure to leave the thinking to Eileen.

One afternoon climbing above the highest camp with Eileen, Roger stands facing out as he belays Eileen's lead up a difficult patch. Thunderheads like long-stemmed mushrooms march in lines blown to

the northeast. Only the tops of the clouds are higher
than they. It is late afternoon and the cliff-face is a
shadow. The cottony trunks of the thunderheads are
dark, shadowed gray—then the thunderheads themselves bulge white and gleaming into the sunny sky
above, actually casting some light back onto the cliff.
Roger pulls the belay rope taut, looks up at Eileen. She
is staring up her line of attack, which has become a
crack in two walls meeting at ninety degrees. Her
oxygen mask covers her mouth and nose. Roger tugs
once—she looks down—he points out at the immense array of clouds. She nods, pulls the mask to one
side. "Like ships!" she calls down. "Ships of the line!"

Roger pulls his mask over a cheek. "Do you think a
storm might come?"

"I wouldn't be surprised. We've been lucky so far."
She replaces her mask and begins a layback, shoving
the fingers of both hands in the crack, putting the soles
of both boots against the wall just below her hands,
and pulling herself out to the side so that she can walk
sideways up one of the walls. Roger keeps the belay
taut.

Mars's prevailing westerlies strike Olympus Mons,
and the air rises, but does not flow over the peak; the
mountain is so tall it protrudes out of much of the
atmosphere, and the winds are therefore pushed
around each side. Compressed in that way, the air
comes swirling off the eastern flank cold and dry,
having dumped its moisture on the western flank,
where glaciers form. This is the usual pattern, anyway;
but when a cyclonic system sweeps out of the southwest, it strikes the volcano a glancing blow from the

south, compresses, lashes the southeast quadrant of
the shield, and rebounds to the east intensified.

"What's the barometer say, Hans?"
"Six hundred millibars."
"You're kidding!"
"That's not too far below normal, actually."
"You're kidding."
"It is low, however. I believe we are being overtaken
by a low-pressure system."

The storm begins as katabatic winds: cold air falling
over the edge of the escarpment and dropping toward
the plain. Sometimes the force of the west wind over
the plateau of the shield blows the gusts out beyond
the actual cliff face, which will then stand in perfect
stillness. But the slight vacuum fills again with a quick
downward blast, that makes the tents boom and
stretch their frames. Roger grunts as one almost
squashes the tent, shaking his head at Eileen. She says,
"Get used to it—there are downdrafts hitting the
upper face more often than not." WHAM! "Although
this one does seem to be a bit stronger than usual. But
it's not snowing, is it?"
Roger looks out the little tent door window.
"Nope."
"Good."
"Awful cold, though." He turns in his sleeping bag.
"That's okay. Snow would be a really bad sign." She
gets on the radio and starts calling around. She and
Roger are in Camp 8 (the cave is now called Camp 6);
Dougal and Frances are in Camp 9, the highest and
most exposed of the new camps; Arthur, Hans, Han-
nah, and Ivan are in Camp 7; and the rest are down in

the cave. They are a little overextended, as Eileen has been loath to pull the last tents out of the cave. Now Roger begins to see why. "Everyone stay inside tomorrow morning until they hear from me at mirror dawn. We'll have another conference then."

The wind rises through the night, and Roger is awakened at three A.M. by a particularly hard blast to the tent. There is very little sound of the wind against the rock—then a BANG and suddenly the tent is whistling and straining like a tortured thing. It lets off and the rocks hoot softly. Settle down and listen to the airy breathing WHAM, the squealing tent is driven down into the niche they have set it in—then sucked back up. The comforting hiss of the oxygen mask, keeping his nose warm for once—WHAM. Eileen is apparently sleeping, her head buried in her sleeping bag; only her bunting cap and the oxygen hose emerge from the drawn-up opening at the top. Roger can't believe the gunshot slaps of the wind don't wake her. He checks his watch, decides it's futile to try falling back asleep. New frost condensation on the inside of the tent falls on his face like snow, scaring him for a moment. But a flashlight gleam directed out the small clear panel in the tent door reveals there is no snow. By the dimmest light of the lamp Roger sets their pot of ice on the square bulk of the stove and turns it on. He puts his chilled hands back in the sleeping bag to watch the stove heat up. Quickly the rings under the pot are a bright orange, palpably radiating heat.

An hour later it is considerably warmer in the tent. Roger sips hot tea, tries to predict the wind's hammering. The melted water from the cave's ice apparently has some silt in it; Roger, along with three or four of the others, has had his digestion upset by the silt, and now he feels a touch of the glacial dysentery coming on. Uncomfortably he quells the urge. Some particularly sharp blows to the tent wake Eileen; she sticks her head out of her bag, looking befuddled.

"Wind's up," Roger says. "Want some tea?"

"Mmmph." She pulls away her oxygen mask. "Yeah." She takes a full cup and drinks. "Thirsty."

"Yeah. The masks seem to do that."

"What time is it?"

"About four."

"Ah. My alarm must have woken me. Almost time for the call."

Although it is cloudy to the east, they still get a distinct increase of light when Archimedes rises. Roger pulls on his cold boots and groans. "Gotta go," he says to Eileen, and unzips the tent just far enough to get out.

"Stay harnessed up!"

Outside, one of the katabatic blasts shoves him hard. It's very cold, perhaps 20 degrees Celsius below, so that the wind chill factor when it is blowing hardest is extreme. Unfortunately, he does have a touch of the runs. Much relieved, and very chilled, he pulls his pants up and steps back into the tent. Eileen is on the radio. People are to stay inside until the winds abate a little, she says. Roger nods vigorously. When she is done she laughs at him. "You know what Dougal would say."

"Oh, it was very invigorating all right."

She laughs again.

Time passes. When he warms back up Roger dozes off. It's actually easier to sleep during the day, when the tent is warmer.

He is rudely awakened late in the morning by a shout from outside. Eileen jerks up in her bag and unzips the tent door. Dougal sticks his head in, pulls his oxygen mask onto his chest, frosts them both with hard breathing. "Our tent has been smashed by a rock," he says, almost apologetically. "Frances has got her arm broke. I need some help getting her down."

"Down where?" Roger says involuntarily.

"Well, I thought to the cave, anyway. Or at least to here—our tent's crushed, she's pretty much out in the open right now—in her bag, you know, but the tent's not doing much."

Grimly Eileen and Roger begin to pull their climbing clothes on.

Outside the wind rips at them and Roger wonders if he can climb. They clip onto the rope and jumar up rapidly, moving at emergency speed. Sometimes the blasts of wind from above are so strong that they can only hang in against the rock and wait. During one blast Roger becomes frightened—it seems impossible that flesh and bone, harness, jumar, rope, piton, and rock will all hold under the immense pressure of the downdraft. But all he can do is huddle in the crack the fixed rope follows and hope, getting colder every second.

They enter a long snaking ice gully that protects them from the worst of the wind, and make better progress. Several times rocks or chunks of ice fall by them, dropping like bombs or giant hailstones. Dougal and Eileen are climbing so fast that it is difficult to keep up with them. Roger feels weak and cold; even though he is completely covered, his nose and fingers feel frozen. His intestines twine a little as he crawls over a boulder jammed in the gully, and he groans. Better to have stayed in the tent on this particular day.

Suddenly they are at Camp 9—one big box tent, flattened at one end. It is flapping like a big flag in a gale, cracking and snapping again and again, nearly drowning out their voices. Frances is glad to see them; under her goggles her eyes are red-rimmed. "I think I can sit up in a sling and rappel down if you can help me," she says over the tent noise.

"How are you?" asks Eileen.

"The left arm's broken just above the elbow. I've made a bit of a splint for it. I'm awfully cold, but other than that I don't feel too bad. I've taken some painkillers, but not enough to make me sleepy."

They all crowd in what's left of the tent and Eileen turns on a stove. Dougal dashes about outside, vainly trying to secure the open end of the tent and end the flapping. They brew tea and sit in sleeping bags to drink it. "What time is it?" "Two." "We'd better be off soon." "Yeah."

Getting Frances down to Camp 8 is slow, cold work. The exertion of climbing the fixed ropes at high speed was just enough to keep them warm on the climb up; now they have to hug the rock and hold on, or wait while Frances is belayed down one of the steeper sections. She uses her right arm and steps down everything she can, helping the process as much as possible.

She is stepping over the boulder that gave Roger such distress, when a blast of wind hits her like a punch, and over the rock she tumbles, face against it.

Roger leaps up from below and grabs her just as she is about to roll helplessly onto her left side. For a moment all he can do is hang there, holding her steady. Dougal and Eileen shout down from above. No room for them. Roger double-sets the jumar on the fixed rope above him, pulls up with one arm, the other around Frances's back. They eye each other through the goggles—she scrambles for a foothold blindly— finds something and takes some of her weight herself. Still, they are stuck there. Roger shows Frances his hand and points at it, trying to convey his plan. She nods. He unclips from the fixed rope, sets the jumar once again right below Frances, descends to a good foothold and laces his hands together. He reaches up, guides Frances's free foot into his hands. She shifts her weight onto that foot and lowers herself until Roger keeps that hold in place. Then the other foot crosses to join Roger's two feet—a good bit of work by Frances, who must be hurting. Mid-move another gust almost wrecks their balance, but they lean into each other and hold. They are below the boulder, and Dougal and Eileen can now climb over it and belay Frances again.

They start down once more. But the exertion has triggered a reaction inside Roger, and suddenly he has to take a shit. He curses the cave silt and tries desperately to quell the urge, but it won't be denied. He signals his need to the others and jumars down the fixed rope away from them, to get out of the way of the descent and obtain a little privacy. Pulling his pants down while the winds drag him around the fixed rope is actually a technical problem, and he curses continuously as he relieves himself. It is without a doubt the coldest shit of his life. By the time the others get to him he is shivering so hard he can barely climb.

They barge into Camp 8 around sunset, and Eileen gets on the radio. The lower camps are informed of the situation and given their instructions. No one questions Eileen when her voice has that edge in it.

The problem is that their camp is low on food and oxygen. "I'll go down and get a load," Dougal says.

"But you've already been out a long time," Eileen says.

"No, no. A hot meal and I'll be off again. You should stay here with Frances, and Roger's chilled down."

"We can get Arthur or Hans to come up."

"We don't want movement up, do we? They'd have to stay up here, and we're out of room as it is. Besides, I'm the most used to climbing in this wind in the dark."

Eileen nods. "Okay."

"You warm enough?" Dougal asks Roger.

Roger can only shiver. They help him into his bag and dose him with tea, but it is hard to drink. Long after Dougal has left he is still shivering.

"Good sign he's shivering," Frances says to Eileen. "But he's awfully cold. Maybe too hypothermic to warm up. I'm cold myself."

Eileen keeps the stove on high till there is a fug of warm air in the tent. She gets into Frances's bag with her, carefully avoiding her injured side. In the ruddy stove light their faces are pinched with discomfort.

"I'm okay," Frances mutters after a while. "Good'n warm. Get him."

Roger is barely conscious as Eileen pushes into his

bag with him. He is resentful that he must move. "Get
your outers off," Eileen orders. They struggle around,
half in the bag, to get Roger's climbing gear off. Lying
together in their thermal underwear, Roger slowly
warms up. "Man, you *are* cold," Eileen says.

"'Preciate it," Roger mutters wearily. "Don't know
what happened."

"We didn't work you hard enough on the descent.
Plus you had to bare your butt to a wind chill factor I
wouldn't want to guess."

Body warmth, seeping into him. Long hard body
pressed against him. She won't let him sleep. "Not
yet. Turn around. Here. Drink this." Frances holds his
eyelids up to check him. "Drink this!" He drinks.
Finally they let him sleep.

Dougal wakes them, barging in with a full pack. He
and the pack are crusted with snow. "Pretty desperate," he says with a peculiar smile. He hurries into a
sleeping bag and drinks tea. Roger checks his watch—
midnight. Dougal has been at it for almost twenty-
four hours, and after wolfing down a pot of stew he
puts on his mask, rolls to a corner of the tent, and falls
into a deep sleep.

Next morning the storm is still battering the tent.
The four of them get ready awkwardly—the tent is
better for three, and they must be careful of Frances's
arm. Eileen gets on the radio and orders those below
to clear Camp 7 and retreat to the cave. Once climbing
they find that Frances's whole side has stiffened up.
Getting her down means they have to hammer in new
pitons, set up rappeling ropes for her, lower her with
one of them jumaring down beside her, while occa-

sionally hunkering down to avoid hard gusts of wind.
They stop in Camp 7 for an hour to rest and eat, then
drop to the cave. It is dusk by the time they enter the
dark refuge.

So they are all back in the cave. The wind swirls in
it, and the others have spent the previous day piling
rocks into the south side of the cave mouth, to build a
protective wall. This helps a bit.

As the fourth day of the storm passes in the whistle
and flap of wind, and an occasional flurry of snow, all
the members of the climb crowd into one of the large
box tents, sitting upright and bumping arms so they
will all fit.

"Look, I don't want to go down just because one of
us has a busted arm," Marie says.

"I can't climb," says Frances. It seems to Roger that
she is holding up very well; her face is white and her
eyes look drugged, but she is quite coherent and very
calm.

"I *know* that," Marie says. "But we could split up.
It'll only take a few people to get you back down to the
cars. The rest of us can take the rest of the gear and
carry on. If we get to the cache at the top of the scarp,
we won't have to worry about supplies. If we don't,
we'll just follow you down. But I don't fancy us giving
up now—that's not what we came for, eh? Going
down when we don't have to?"

Eileen looks at Ivan. "It'd be up to you to get
Frances down."

Ivan grimaces, nods. "That's what Sherpas are for,"
he says gamely.

"Do you think four will be enough for it?"

"More would probably just get in the way."

There is a quick discussion of their supply situation. Hans is of the opinion that they are short enough on supplies to make splitting up dangerous. "It seems to me that our primary responsibility is to get Frances to the ground safely. The climb can be finished another time."

Marie argues with this, but Hans is supported by Stephan, and it seems neither side will convince the other. After an apprehensive silence, Eileen clears her throat.

"Marie's plan sounds good to me," she says briefly. "We've got the supplies to go both ways, and the Sherpas can get Frances down by themselves."

"Neither groups will have much margin for error," Hans says.

"We can leave the water for the group going down," Marie says. "There'll be ice and snow the rest of the way up."

"We'll have to be a bit more sparing with the oxygen," Hans says. "Frances should have enough to take her all the way down."

"Yes," Eileen says. "We'll have to get going again in the next day or two, no matter what the weather's like."

"Well?" says Marie. "We've proved that we can get up and down the fixed ropes in any weather. We should get up and fix Camp 9 as soon as we can. Tomorrow, say."

"If there's a bit of a break."

"We've got to stock the higher camps—"

"Yeah. We'll do what we can, Marie. Don't fret."

While the storm continues they make preparations to split up. Roger, who wants to stay clear of all that,

helps Arthur to build the wall at the cave's entrance.
They have started at the southern end, filling up the
initial crack of the cave completely. After that they
must be satisfied with a two-meter high wall, which
they extend across the entrance until the boulders on
the floor of the cave are used up. Then they sit against
the wall and watch the division of the goods. Wind
still whistles through the cave, but sitting at the
bottom of the wall they can feel that they did some
good.

The division of equipment is causing some problems. Marie is very possessive about the oxygen
bottles: "Well, you'll be going down, right?" she
demands of Ivan. "You don't need oxygen at all once
you get a couple camps down."

"Frances will need it longer than that," Ivan said.
"And we can't be sure how long it'll take to get her
down."

"Hell, you can *reel* her down once you get past the
Thank God Ledge. Shouldn't take you any time at
all—"

"Marie, get out of this," Eileen snaps. "We'll divide
the supplies—there's no reason for you to bother with
this."

Marie glares, stomps off to her tent.

Arthur and Roger give each other the eye. The
division goes on. Rope will be the biggest problem, it
appears. But everything will be tight.

At the first break in the winds the rescue party—
Frances and the four Sherpas—take off. Roger de-
scends with them to help them cross the Thank God
Ledge, and to recover the fixed rope there. The wind

still gusts, but with less violence. In the middle of the ledge crossing Frances loses her balance and swings around; Roger reaches her (not noticing he ran) and holds her in. "We have to stop meeting like this," Frances says, voice muffled by her mask.

When they reach the Great Gully, Roger says his good-byes. The Sherpas are cheery enough, but Frances is white-faced and quiet. She has said hardly a word in the last couple of days, and Roger cannot tell what she is thinking. "Bad luck," he tells her. "You'll get another chance, though."

"Thanks for grabbing me during the descent from Camp 9," she says just as he is about to leave. She looks upset. "You're awfully quick. That would have hurt like hell if I had rolled onto my left side."

"I'm glad I could help," Roger says. Then, as he leaves: "I like how tough you've been."

A grimace from Frances.

On the way back Roger must free the fixed rope to recover it for the climb above, and so on the Thank God Ledge he is always belayed only to the piton ahead. If he were to fall he would drop—sometimes up to twenty-five meters—and swing like a pendulum over the rough basalt. The ledge becomes new again; he finds that the smooth surface of the sidewalk is indeed wide enough to walk on, but still—the wind pushes at his back—he is alone—the sky is low and dark, and threatens to snow—and all of a sudden the hair on his neck rises, the oxygen whistles in his mask as he sucks it down, the pitted rock face seems to glow with an internal light of its own, and all the world expands, expands ever outward, growing more immense with every pulse of his blood; and his lungs fill, and fill, and fill. . . .

Back in the cave Roger says nothing about the eerie moment on the ledge. Only Eileen and Hans are still in the cave—the others have gone up to supply the higher camps, and Dougal and Marie have gone all the way up to Camp 9. Eileen, Hans and Roger load up their packs—very heavy loads, they find when they duck out the cave—and start up the fixed ropes. Jumaring up the somewhat icy rope is difficult, in places dangerous. The wind strikes from the left now rather than from above. By the time they reach Camp 7 it is nearly dark, and Stephan and Arthur already occupy the single tent. In the mirror dusk and the strong side wind, erecting another tent is no easy task. There is not another level spot to set it on, either— they must place it on a slope, and tie it to pitons hammered into the cliff. By the time Eileen and Roger and Hans get into the new tent, Roger is freezing and starving and immensely tired. "Pretty bloody desperate," he says wearily, mimicking Marie and the Sherpas. They melt snow and cook up a pot of stew from their sleeping bags, and when they are done eating, Roger puts on his oxygen mask, sets the flow for sleep, and slumps off.

The moment on the Thank God Ledge jumps to his mind and wakes him momentarily. Wind whips the taut walls of the tent, and Eileen, pencilling logistic notes for the next day, slides down the slope under the tent until their two sleeping bags are one clumped mass. Roger looks at her: brief smile from that tired, puffy, frost-burned face. Great deltas of wrinkles under her eyes. His feet begin to warm up and he falls asleep to the popping of the tent, the hiss of oxygen, the scratching of a pencil.

That night the storm picks up again.

The next morning they take down the tent in a strong wind—hard work—and start portering loads up to Camp 8. Halfway between camps it begins to snow. Roger watches his feet through swirls of hard dry granules. His gloved fingers twist around the frigid jumar, sliding it up the frosted rope, clicking it home, pulling himself up. It is a struggle to see footholds in the spindrift, which moves horizontally across the cliff face, from left to right as he looks at it. The whole face appears to be whitely streaming to the side, like a wave. He finds he must focus his attention entirely on his hands and feet. His fingers, nose and toes are very cold. He rubs his nose through the mask, feels nothing. The wind pushes him hard, like a giant trying to make him fall. In the narrow gullies the wind is less strong, but they find themselves climbing up through waves of avalanching snow, drift after drift of it piling up between their bodies and the slope, burying them, sliding between their legs and away. One gully seems to last forever. Intermittently Roger is concerned about his nose, but mostly he worries about his immediate situation: moving up the rope, keeping a foothold. Visibility is down to about fifty meters— they are in a little white bubble flying to the left through white snow, or so it appears.

At one point Roger must wait for Eileen and Hans to get over the boulder that Frances had such trouble with. His mind wanders and it occurs to him that their chances of success have shifted radically—and with them, the nature of the climb. Low on supplies, facing an unknown route in deteriorating weather—Roger wonders how Eileen will handle it. She has led expeditions before, but this kind only comes about by accident.

She passes him going strong, beats ice from the ropes, sweeps spindrift from the top of the boulder. Pulls up over it in one smooth motion. The wind cuts through Roger as he watches Hans repeat the operation: cuts through the laminated outer suit, the thick bunting inner suit, his skin. . . . He brushes spindrift from his goggles with a frigid hand and heaves up after them.

Though it is spring, the winter-like low-pressure system over Olympus Mons is in place, drawing the wet winds up from the south, creating stable storm conditions on the south and east arcs of the escarpment. The snow is irregular, the winds constant. For the better part of a week the seven climbers left on the face struggle in the miserable conditions. One night at sunset radio hour they hear from Frances and the Sherpas, down at base camp. There is a lot of sand in Martian snow, and their voices are garbled by static, but the message is clear: they are down, they are safe, they are leaving for Alexandria to get Frances's arm set. Roger catches on Eileen's averted face an expression of pure relief, and realizes that her silence in the past few days has been a manifestation of worry. Now, looking pleased, she gives the remaining climbers their instructions for the next day, in a fresh, determined tone.

Into camp at night, cold and almost too tired to walk. Big loaded packs onto the various ledges and niches that serve for this particular camp. Hands shaking with hunger. This camp—number 13, Roger believes—is on a saddle between two ridges overlooking a deep, twisted chimney. "Just like the Devil's Kitchen on Ben Nevis," Arthur remarks when they get inside the tent. He eats with gusto. Roger shivers and puts his hands two centimeters above the glowing stove ring. Transferring from climbing mode to tent mode is a tricky business, and tonight Roger hasn't done so well. At this altitude and in these winds, cold has become their most serious opponent. Overmitts off, and everything must be done immediately to get lightly gloved hands protected again as quickly as possible. Even if the rest of one's body is warmed by exertion, the fingertips will freeze within a few minutes. Yet so many camp operations can be done easier with hands out of mitts. Frostnip is the frequent result, leaving the fingers tender, so that pulling up a rockface, or even buttoning or zipping one's clothes, becomes a painful task. Frostnip blisters kill the skin, creating black patches that take a week or more to peel away. Now when they sit in the tents around the ruddy light of the stove, observing solemnly the progress of the cooking meal, they see across the pot faces blotched on cheek or nose: black skin peeling away to reveal new skin beneath. . . .

They climb onto a band of rotten rock, a tuff and lava composite that sometimes breaks off right in their hands. It takes Marie and Dougal two full days to find decent belay points for the hundred and fifty meters of the band, and every morning the rockfall is frequent and frightening. "It's a bit like swimming up the thing, isn't it?" Dougal comments. When they make it to the hard rock above, Eileen orders Dougal and Marie to the bottom of their "ladder," to get some rest. Marie makes no complaint now; each day in the lead is an exhausting exercise, and Marie and Dougal are beat.

Every night Eileen works out plans for the following day, revising them as conditions and the climbers' strength and health change. The logistics are complicated, and each day the seven climbers shift partners and positions in the climb. Eileen scribbles in her notebook and jabbers on the radio every dusk, altering the schedules and changing her orders with almost every new bit of information she receives from the higher camps. Her method appears chaotic. Marie dubs her the "Mad Mahdi," and scoffs at the constant change in plans; but she obeys them, and they work: every night they are scattered in two or three camps up and down the cliff, with everything they need to survive the night, and get them higher the next day; and every new day they leap-frog up, pulling out the lowest camp, finding a place to establish a new high camp. The bitter winds continue. Everything is difficult. They lose track of camp numbers, and name them only high, middle, and low.

Naturally, three quarters of everyone's work is portering—carrying heavy loads up the fixed ropes of routes already established. Roger begins to feel that he is surviving the rigors of the weather and altitude better than most of the rest; he can carry more faster, and even though most days end in that state where each step is ten breaths' agony, he finds he can take on more the next day. His digestion returns to normal, which is a blessing—a great physical pleasure, in fact. Perhaps improvement in this area masks the effects of altitude, or perhaps the altitude isn't bothering Roger yet; it is certainly true that high altitude affects people differently, for reasons unconnected with basic strength—in fact, for reasons not yet fully understood.

So Roger becomes the chief porter; Dougal calls him Roger Sherpa, and Arthur calls him Tenzing. The day's challenge becomes to do all the myriad activities of the day as efficiently as possible, without frostnip, without excessive discomfort, hunger, thirst, or exhaustion. He hums to himself little snatches of music. His favorite is the eight-note phrase repeated by the basses near the end of the first movement of Beethoven's Ninth: six notes down, two notes up, over and over and over. And each evening in the sleeping bag, warm, well-fed, and prone, is a little victory.

One night he wakes up to darkness and silence, fully awake in an instant, heart pounding. Confused, he thinks he may have dreamt of the Thank God Ledge. But then he notices the silence again and realizes his oxygen bottle has run out. It happens every week or so. He uncouples the bottle from the regulator, finds another bottle in the dark and clips it in place. When he tells Arthur about it next morning, Arthur laughs. "That happened to me a couple of nights ago. I don't think anybody could sleep through their oxygen bottle running out—I mean you wake up *very* awake, don't you?"

In the hard rock band Roger porters up a pitch that leaves him whistling into his mask: the gullies have disappeared, above is a nearly vertical black wall, and breaking it is one lightning bolt crack, now marked by a fixed rope with slings attached, making it a sort of rope ladder. Fine for him, but the lead climb! "Must have been Dougal at it again."

And the next day he is out on the lead himself with Arthur, on a continuation of the same face. Leading is very unlike portering. Suddenly the dogged, repetitious, almost mindless work of carrying loads is replaced by the anxious attentiveness of the lead. Arthur takes the first pitch and finishes it bubbling over with enthusiasm. Only his oxygen mask keeps him from carrying on a long conversation as Roger takes over the lead. Then Roger is up there himself, above the last belay on empty rock, looking for the best way. The lure of the lead returns, the pleasure of the problem solved fills him with energy. Fully back in lead mode, he collaborates with Arthur—who turns out to be an ingenious and resourceful technical climber—on the best storm day yet: five hundred meters of fixed rope, their entire supply, nailed up in one day. They hurry back down to camp and find Eileen and Marie still there, dumping food for the next few days.

"By God are we a team!" Arthur cries as they describe the day's work. "Eileen, you should put us together more often. Don't you agree, Roger?"

Roger grins at Eileen, nods. "That was fun."

Marie and Eileen leave for the camp below, and Arthur and Roger cook a big pot of stew and trade climbing stories, scores of them: and every one ends, "but that was nothing compared to today."

Heavy snow returns and traps them in their tents, and it's all they can do to keep the high camp supplied. "Bloody desperate out!" Marie complains, as if she can't believe how bad it is. After one bad afternoon Stephan and Arthur are in the high camp, Eileen and Roger in the middle camp, and Hans, Marie, and Dougal in the low camp with all the supplies. The storm strikes Roger and Eileen's tent so hard that they are considering bringing in some rocks to weight it down more. A buzz sounds from their radio and Eileen picks it up.

"Eileen, this is Arthur. I'm afraid Stephan has come up too fast."

Eileen scowls fearfully, swears under her breath. Stephan has gone from low camp to the high one in two hard day's climbing.

"He's very short of breath, and he's spitting up bloody spit. And talking like a madman."

"I'm okay!" Stephan shouts through the static. "I'm fine!"

"Shut up! You're not fine! Eileen, did you hear that? I'm afraid he's got edema."

"Yeah," Eileen says. "Has he got a headache?"

"No. It's just his lungs right now. I think. Shut up! I can hear his chest bubbling, you know."

"Yeah. Pulse up?"

"Pulse weak and rapid, yeah."

"Damn." Eileen looks over at Roger. "Put him on maximum oxygen."

"I already have. Still . . ."

"I know. We've got to get him down."

"I'm okay!"

"Yeah," Arthur says. "He needs to come down, at least to your camp, maybe lower."

"Damn it," Eileen exclaims when off the radio. "I moved him up too fast."

An hour later—calls made below, the whole group

in action—Roger and Eileen are out in the storm
again, in the dark, their helmet headlights showing
them only a portion of the snowfall. They cannot
afford to wait until morning—pulmonary edema can
be quickly fatal, and the best treatment by far is to get
the victim lower, where his lungs can clear out the
excess water. Even a small drop in altitude can make a
dramatic difference. So off they go; Roger takes the
lead and bashes ice from the rope, jumars up, scrab-
bles over the rock blindly with his crampon-tips to get
a purchase in the snow and ice. It is bitterly cold, and
his goggles allow the cold onto his eyes. They reach
the bottom of the blank wall pitch that so impressed
Roger, and the going is treacherous. He wonders how
they will get Stephan down it. The fixed rope is the
only thing making the ascent possible, but it does less
and less to aid them as ice coats it and the rock face.
Wind hammers them, and Roger has a sudden acute
sensation of the empty space behind them. The head-
light beams reveal only swirling snow. Fear adds its
own kind of chill to the mix. . . .

By the time they reach high camp Stephan is quite
ill. No more protests from him. "I don't know how
we'll get him down," Arthur says anxiously. "I gave
him a small shot of morphine to get the peripheral
veins to start dilating."

"Good. We'll just have to truss him into a harness
and lower him."

"Easier said than done, in this stuff."

Stephan is barely conscious, coughing and hacking
with every breath. Pulmonary edema fills the lungs
with water; unless the process is reversed, he will
drown. Just getting him into the sling (another function of the little wall tents) is hard work. Then outside

again—struck by the wind—and to the fixed ropes. Roger descends first, Eileen and Arthur lower Stephan using a power reel, and Roger collects him like a large bundle of laundry. After standing him upright and knocking the frozen spittle from the bottom of his mask, Roger waits for the other two, and when they arrive he starts down again. The descent seems endless, and everyone gets dangerously cold. Wind-blown snow, the rock face, omnipresent cold: nothing else in the world. At the end of one drop Roger cannot undo the knot at the end of his belay line, to send it back up for Stephan. For fifteen minutes he struggles with the frozen knot, which resembles a wet iron pretzel. Nothing to cut it off with, either. For a while it seems they will all freeze because he can't untie a knot. Finally he takes his climbing gloves off and pulls at the thing with his bare fingers until it comes loose.

Eventually they arrive at the lower camp, where Hans and Dougal are waiting with a medical kit. Stephan is zipped into a sleeping bag, and given a diuretic and some more morphine. Rest and the drop in altitude should see him back to health, although at the moment his skin is blue and his breathing ragged: no guarantees. He could die—a man who might live a thousand years—and suddenly their whole enterprise seems crazy. His coughs sound weak behind the oxygen mask, which hisses madly on maximum flow.

"He should be okay," Hans pronounces. "Won't know for sure for several hours."

But there they are—seven people in two wall tents. "We'll go back up," Eileen says, looking to Roger. He nods.

* * *

And they go back out again. The swirl of white snow
in their headlights, the buffets of wind . . . they are
tired, and progress is slow. Roger slips once and the
jumars don't catch on the icy rope for about three
meters, where they suddenly catch and test his harness, and the piton above. A fall! The spurt of fear
gives him a second wind. Stubbornly he decides that
much of his difficulty is mental. It's dark and windy,
but really the only difference between this and his
daytime climbs during the last week is the cold, and
the fact that he can't see much. But the helmet lamps
do allow him to see—he is at the center of a shifting
white sphere, and the rock he must work on is
revealed. It is covered with a sheet of ice and impacted
snow, and where the ice is clear it gleams in the light
like glass laid over the black rock beneath. Crampons
are great in this—the sharp front points stick in the
snow and ice firmly, and the only problem is the
brittle black glass that will break away from the points
in big jagged sheets. Even black ice can be distinguished in the bright bluish gleam of the lights, so the
work is quite possible. Look at it as just another
climb, he urges himself, meanwhile kicking like a
maniac with his left foot to spike clear a crack where
he can nail in another piton to replace a bad hold. The
dizzying freeness of a pull over an outcropping; the
long reach up for a solid knob: he becomes aware of
the work as a sort of game, a set of problems to be
solved despite cold or thirst or fatigue (his hands are
beginning to tire from the long night's hauling, so that
each hold hurts). Seen this way, it all changes. Now
the wind is an opponent to be beaten, but also to be
respected. The same of course is true of the rock, his

principal opponent—and this a daunting one, an opponent to challenge him to his utmost performance. He kicks into a slope of hard snow and ascends rapidly.

He looks down as Eileen kicks up the slope: quick reminder of the stakes of this game. The light on the top of her helmet makes her look like a night insect, or a deep sea fish. She reaches him quickly; one long gloved hand over the wall's top, and she joins him with a smooth contraction of the bicep. Strong woman, Roger thinks, but decides to take another lead anyway. He is in a mood now where he doubts anyone but Dougal could lead as fast.

Up through the murk they climb.

An odd point is that the two climbers can scarcely communicate. Roger "hears" Eileen through varieties of tugging on the rope linking them. If he takes too long to study a difficult spot above, he feels a mild interrogatory tug on the rope. Two tugs when Roger is belaying means she's on her way up. Very taut belaying betrays her belief that he is in a difficult section. So communication by rope can be fairly complex and subtle. But aside from it, and the infrequent shout with the mask pulled up to one side (which includes the punishment of a face full of spindrift) they are isolated. Mute partners. The exchange of lead goes well—one passes the other with a wave—the belay is ready. Up Eileen goes. Roger watches and holds the belay taut. Little time for contemplating their situation, thankfully; but while taking a rest on crampon points in steps chopped out with his ice axe, Roger feels acutely the *thereness* of his position, cut off from past or future, irrevocably in this moment, on this cliff face that drops away bottomlessly, extends up forever. Unless he climbs well, there will never be any other reality.

Then they reach a pitch where the fixed rope has been cut in the middle. Falling rock or ice has shaved it off. A bad sign. Now Roger must climb a ropeless pitch, hammering in pitons on his way to protect himself. Every meter above the last belay is two meters fall. . . .

Roger never expected this hard a climb, and adrenaline banishes his exhaustion. He studies the first small section of a pitch that he knows is ten or twelve meters long, invisible in the dark snow flurries above. Probably Marie or Dougal climbed this crack the first time. He discovers that the crack just gives him room for his hands. Almost a vertical crack for a while, with steps cut into the ice. Up he creeps, crab-like and sure-footed. Now the crack widens and the ice is too far back in it to be of use—but the cramponed boots can be stuck in the crack and turned sideways, to stick tenuously into the thin ice coating the crack's interior. One creates one's own staircase, mostly using the tension of the twisted crampons. Now the crack abruptly closes and he has to look around, ah, there, a horizontal crack holding the empty piton. Very good —he hooks into it and is protected thus far. Perhaps the next piton is up this rampway to the right? Clawing to find the slight indentations that pass for handholds here, crouching to lean up the ramp in a tricky walk—he wonders about the crampons here . . . ah. The next piton, right at eye level. Perfect. And then an area lined with horizontal strata about a

meter in thickness, making a steep—a very steep—
ladder.

And at the top of that pitch they find the high camp
tent, crushed under a load of snow. Avalanche. One
corner of the tent flaps miserably.

Eileen comes up and surveys the damage in the
double glare of their two headlamps. She points at the
snow, makes a digging motion. The snow is so cold
that it can't bind together—moving it is like kicking
coarse sand. They get to work, having no other choice.
Eventually the tent is free, and as an added benefit
they are warmed as well, although Roger feels he can
barely move. The tent's poles have been bent and
some broken, and splints must be tied on before the
tent can be redeployed. Roger kicks snow and ice
chunks around the perimeter of the tent, until it is
"certifiably bombproof," as the leads would say. Except if another avalanche hits it . . . something they
can't afford to think about, as they can't move the
camp anywhere else. They simply have to risk it.
Inside, they drop their packs and start the stove and
put a pot of ice on. Then crampons off, and into
sleeping bags. With the bags around them up to the
waist, they can start sorting out the mess. There is
spindrift on everything, but unless it gets right next to
the stove it will not melt. Digging in the jumbled piles
of gear for a packet of stew, Roger feels again how
tired his body is. Oxygen masks off, so they can drink.
"That was quite an excursion." Raging thirst. They
laugh with relief. He brushes an unused pot with his
bare hand, guaranteeing a frostnip blister. Eileen
calculates the chance of another avalanche without
trepidation: ". . . so if the wind stays high enough we

should be okay." They discuss Stephan, and sniff like hunting dogs at the first scent of the stew. Eileen digs out the radio and calls down to the low camp. Stephan is sleeping, apparently without discomfort. "Morphine will do that," Eileen says. They wolf down their meal in a few minutes.

The snow under the tent is torn up by boot prints, and Roger's sleeping surface is unbelievably lumpy. He rolls over until he is wedged against the length of Eileen's bag, coveting the warmth and hoping for a flatter surface. It is just as lumpy there. Eileen snuggles back into him and he can feel the potential for warmth; he can tell he will warm up. He wonders if getting into one bag would be worth the effort.

"Amazing what some people will do for fun," Eileen comments drowsily.

Short laugh. "This isn't the fun part."

"Isn't it? That climb . . ."

Big yawn. "That was some climb," he agrees. No denying it.

"That was a great climb."

"Especially since we didn't get killed."

"Yeah." She yawns too, and Roger can feel a great wave of sleep about to break over him and sweep him away. "I hope Stephan gets better. Otherwise we'll have to take him down."

In the next few days everyone has to go out several times in the storm, to keep the high camp supplied and to keep the fixed ropes free of ice. The work is miserable when they can do it, and sometimes they can't: the wind on some days shuts down everything, and they can only huddle inside and hope the tents hold to the face. One dim day Roger is sitting with Stephan and Arthur in low camp. Stephan has recovered from the edema, and is anxious to climb again. "No hurry," Roger says. "No one's going anywhere anyway, and water in the lungs is serious business. You'll have to take it slow—"

The tent door is unzipped and a plume of snow enters, followed by Dougal. He grins hello. The silence seems to call for some comment: "Pretty invigorating out there," he says to fill it, and looks after a pot of tea. The shy moment having passed he chats cheerfully with Arthur about the weather. Tea done, he is off again; he is in a hurry to get a load up to the high camp. A quick grin and he is out the tent and gone. And it occurs to Roger that there are two types of climber on their expedition (another duality): those who *endure* the bad weather and accidents and all the various difficulties of the face that are making this climb so uncomfortable; and those who, in some important, peculiar way, *enjoy* all the trouble. In the former group are Eileen, who has the overriding responsibility for the climb—Marie, who is in such a hurry for the top—and Hans and Stephan, who are less experienced and would be just as happy to climb under sunny skies and with few serious difficulties. Each of these is steady and resolute, without a doubt; but they endure.

Dougal, on the other hand, Dougal and Arthur: these two are quite clearly *enjoying* themselves, and the worse things get the more fun they seem to have. It is, Roger thinks, perverse. The reticent, solitary Dougal, seizing with quiet glee every possible chance to get out in the gale and climb. . . . "He certainly seems to be enjoying himself," Roger says out loud, and Arthur laughs.

"That Dougal!" he cries. "What a Brit he is. You know climbers are the same everywhere. I come all the way to Mars and find just the people you'd expect to find on Ben Nevis. Course it stands to reason, doesn't it? That New Scotland school and all."

It is true; from the very start of the colonization British climbers have been coming to Mars in search of new climbs, and many of them have stayed.

"And I'll tell you," Arthur continues, "those guys are never happier than when it's blowing force ten and dumping snow by the dumptruck. Or not snow, actually. More like sleet, that's what they want. One degree rain, or wet snow. Perfect. And you know why they want it? So they can come back in at the end of the day and say, 'Bloody desperate out today, eh mate?' They're all dying to be able to say that. 'Bluidy *das*perate, mite.' Ha! Do you know what I mean? It's like giving themselves a medal or something, I don't know."

Roger and Stephan, smiling, nod. "Very macho," Stephan says.

"But Dougal!" Arthur cries. "Dougal! He's too cool for that. He goes out there in the nastiest conditions he can possibly find—I mean look at him just now— he couldn't *wait* to get back out there! Didn't want to waste such a fine opportunity! And he climbs the hardest pitches he can find, too. Have you seen him? You've seen the routes he leaves behind. Man, that guy could climb buttered glass in a hurricane. And what does he say about it? Does he say that was pretty bloody desperate? No! he says," and Roger and Stephan join in, like a chorus: "How invigorating!"

"Yeah," Stephan says, laughing. "Pretty invigorating out there, all right."

"The Scots," Arthur says, giggling away. "Martian Scots, no less. I can't believe it."

"It's not just the Scots are strange," Roger points out. "What about you, Arthur? I notice you getting quite a giggle out of all this yourself, eh?"

"Oh, yeah, yeah," Arthur says. "I'm having a good time. Aren't you? I'll tell you, once we got on the oxygen I started feeling great. Before that it wasn't so easy. The air seemed really thin, I mean *really* thin. Elevations here don't mean anything to me, I mean you haven't got a sea level so what does elevation really mean, right? But your air is like nothing, man. So when we got on the bottle I could really feel the difference. A lifesaver. And then there's the gravity! Now that's wonderful. What is it, two fifths of a gee? Practically nothing! You might as well be on the moon! As soon as I learned to balance properly, I really started to have a good time. Felt like Superman. On this planet it just isn't that hard to go uphill, that's all." He laughs, toasts the other two with tea: "On Mars, I'm Superman."

High altitude pulmonary edema works fast, and one either succumbs or recovers very quickly. When Stephan's lungs are completely clear Hans orders him to keep on maximum oxygen intake, and he is given a light load and ordered to take it slow and only move up from one low camp to the next. At this point, Roger thinks, it would be more difficult to get him back down the cliff than keep on going to the top; a common enough climbing situation, but one that no one talks about. Stephan complains about his reduced role, but agrees to go along with it. For his first few days back out Roger teams with him and keeps a sharp eye on him. But Stephan climbs fairly rapidly, and only complains at Roger's solicitousness, and at the cold winds. Roger concludes he is all right.

Back to portering. Hans and Arthur are out in the lead, having a terrible time with a broad, steep rampart that they are trying to force directly. For a couple of days they are all stalled as the camps are stocked, and the lead party cannot make more than fifty or seventy-five meters a day. One evening on the radio while Hans describes a difficult overhang, Marie gets on the horn and starts in. "Well, I don't know what's going on up there, but with Stephan sucking down the oxygen and you all making centimeters a day we're going to end up stuck on this damn cliff for good! What? I don't give a fuck *what* your troubles are, mate—if you can't make the lead you should bloody well get down and let somebody on there who can!"

"This is a big tuff band," Arthur says defensively. "Once we get above this it's more or less a straight shot to the top—"

"If you've got any bloody oxygen it is! Look, what is this, a co-op? I didn't join a fucking co-op!"

Roger watches Eileen closely. She is listening carefully to the exchange, her finger on the intercom, a deep furrow between her eyes, as if she is concentrating. He is surprised she has not already intervened. But she lets Marie get off another couple of blasts, and only then does she cut in: "Marie! Marie! Eileen here—"

"I know that."

"Arthur and Hans are scheduled to come down soon. Meanwhile, shut up."

And the next day, Arthur and Hans put up three hundred meters of fixed rope, and top the tuff band. When Hans announces this on the sunset radio call (Roger can just hear Arthur in the background, saying in falsetto "So there! So there!"), a little smile twitches Eileen's mouth, before she congratulates them and gets on to the orders for the next day. Roger nods thoughtfully.

After they get above Hans and Arthur's band, the slope lays back a bit and progress is more rapid, even in the continuous winds. The cliff here is like a wall of immense irregular bricks which have been shoved back, so that each brick is set a bit behind the one below it. This great jumble of blocks and ledges and ramps makes for easy zig-zag climbing, and good campsites. One day, Roger stops for a break and looks around. He is portering a load from middle camp to high camp, and has gotten ahead of Eileen. No one in sight. There is a cloud layer far below them, a grey rumpled blanket covering the whole world. Then there is the vertical realm of the cliff-face, a crazed jumble of a block-wall, which extends up to a very smooth, almost featureless cloud layer above them. Only the finest ripples, like waves, mar this grey ceiling. Floor and ceiling of cloud, wall of rock: it seems for a moment that this climb will go on eternally, it is a whole world, an infinite wall that they will climb forever. When has it been any different? Sandwiched like this, between cloud and cloud, it is easy not to believe in the past; perhaps the planet is a cliff, endlessly varied, endlessly challenging.

Then in the corner of Roger's eye, a flash of color. He looks at the deep crack between the ledge he is standing on and the next vertical block. In the twisted ice nestles a patch of moss campion. Cushion of black-green moss, a circle of perhaps a hundred tiny dark pink flowers on it. After three weeks of almost unrelieved black and white, the color seems to burst out of the flowers and explode in his eyes. Such a dark, intense pink! Roger crouches to inspect them. The moss is very finely textured, and appears to be growing directly out of the rock, although no doubt there is some sand back in the crack. A seed or a scrap of moss must have been blown off the shield plateau and down the cliff, to take root here.

Roger stands, looks around again. Eileen has joined him, and she observes him sharply. He pulls his mask to the side. "Look at that," he says. "You can't get away from it anywhere!"

She shakes her head. Pulls her mask down. "It's not the new landscape you hate so much," she says. "I saw the way you were looking at that plant. And it's just a plant, after all, doing its best to live. No, I think you've made a displacement. You use topography as a symbol. It's not the landscape, it's the people. It's the history we've made that you dislike. The terraforming is just part of it—the visible sign of a history of exploitation."

Roger considers it. "We're just another Terran colony, you mean. Colonialism——"

"Yes! That's what you hate, see? Not topography, but history. Because the terraforming, so far, is a waste. It's not being done for any good purpose."

Uneasily Roger shakes his head. He has not thought

of it like that, and isn't sure he completely agrees: it's the land that has suffered the most, after all. Although—

Eileen continues: "There's some good in that, if you think about it. Because the landscape isn't going to change back, ever. But history—history must change, by definition."

And she takes the lead, leaving Roger to stare up after her.

The winds die in the middle of the night. The cessation of tent noise wakes Roger up. It is bitterly cold, even in his bag. It takes him a while to figure out what woke him; his oxygen is still hissing softly in his face. When he figures out what did it, he smiles. Checking his watch, he finds it is almost time for the mirror dawn. He sits up and turns on the stove for tea. Eileen stirs in her sleeping bag, opens one eye. Roger likes watching her wake; even behind the mask, the shift from vulnerable girl to expedition leader is easy to see. It's like ontogeny recapitulating phylogeny: coming to consciousness in the morning recapitulates maturation in life. Now all he needs is the Greek terminology, and he will have a scientific truth. Eileen pulls off her oxygen mask and rolls onto one elbow.

"Want some tea?" he says.

"Yeah."

"It'll be a moment."

"Hold the stove steady—I've got to pee." She stands in the tent doorway, sticks a plastic urine scoop into the open fly of her pants, urinates out the door. "Wow! Sure is cold out. And clear! I can see stars."

"Great. The wind's died, too, see?"

Eileen crawls back into her bag. They brew their tea with great seriousness, as if mixing delicate elixirs. Roger watches her drink.

"Do you really not remember us from before?" he asks.

"Nooo . . ." Eileen says slowly. "We were in our twenties, right? No, the first years I really remember are from my fifties, when I was training up in the caldera. Wall climbs, kind of like this, actually." She sips. "But tell me about us."

Roger shrugs. "It doesn't matter."

"It must be odd. To remember when the rest don't."

"Yes, it is."

"I was probably awful at that age."

"No, no. You were fine."

She laughs. "I can't believe that. Unless I've gone downhill since then."

"Not at all! You sure couldn't have done all this back then."

"I believe that. Getting half an expedition strung out all over a cliff, people sick—"

"No, no. You're doing fine."

She shakes her head. "You can't pretend this climb has gone well. I remember that much."

"What hasn't gone well hasn't been your fault, as you must admit. In fact, given what has happened, we're doing very well, I think. And that's mostly your doing. Not easy with Frances and Stephan, and the storm, and Marie."

"Marie!"

They laugh. "And this storm," Roger says. "That night climb we did, getting Stephan down!" He sips his tea.

"That was a wild one," Eileen says firmly.

Roger nods. They have that. He gets up to pee himself, letting in a blast of intensely cold air. "My God that's cold! What's the temperature?"

"Sixty below, outside."

"Oh. No wonder. I guess that cloud cover was doing us *some* good." Outside it is still dark, and the ice-bearded cliff-face gleams whitely under the stars.

"I like the way you lead the expedition," Roger says into the tent as he zips up. "It's a very light touch, but you still have things under control."

Only slurping sounds from Eileen. Roger zips the tent door closed and hustles back into his bag.

"More tea?" she asks.

"Definitely."

"Here—roll back here, you'll warm up faster, and I could use the insulation myself." Roger nods, shivering, and rolls his bag into the back side of hers, so they are both on one elbow, spooned together.

They sip tea and talk. Roger warms up, stops shivering. Pleasure of empty bladder, of contact with her. They finish the tea and doze for a bit in the warmth. Keeping the oxygen masks off prevents them from falling into a deep sleep. "Mirrors'll be up soon." "Yeah." "Here—move over a bit." Roger remembers when they were lovers, so long ago. Previous lifetime. She was the city dweller then, he the canyon crawler. Now . . . now all the comfort, warmth and contact have given him an erection. He wonders if she can feel it through the two bags. Probably not. Hmmm. He remembers suddenly—the first time they made love was in a tent. He went to bed, and she came right into his little cubicle of the communal tent and jumped him! Remembering it does nothing to make his erection go away. He won-

ders if he can get away with a similar sort of act here.
They are definitely pressed together hard. All that
climbing together: Eileen pairs the climbing teams, so
she must have enjoyed it too. And climbing together
has that sort of dance-like teamwork—boulder ballet;
and the constant kinetic juxtaposition, the felt relationship of the rope, has a certain sensuousness to it.
It is a physical partnership, without a doubt. Of
course all this can be true and climbing remain a
profoundly non-sexual relationship—there are certainly other things to think about. But now . . .

Now she is dozing again. He thinks about her
climbing, her leadership. The things she said to him
back down in the first camps, when he was so depressed. A sort of teacher, really.

Thoughts of that lead him to memories of his past,
of the failed work. For the first time in many days his
memory presents him with the usual parade of the
past, the theater of ghosts. How can he ever assume
such a long and fruitless history? Is it even possible?

Mercifully the tea's warmth, and the mere fact of
lying prone, have their way with him, and he dozes off
himself.

The day dawns. Sky like a sheet of old paper, the
sun a big bronze coin below them to the east. The sun!
Wonderful to see sunlight, shadows. In the light the
cliff face looks sloped back an extra few degrees, and it
seems there is an end to it up there. Eileen and Roger
are in the middle camp, and after ferrying a load to
the high camp they follow the rope's zig-zag course up
the narrow ledges. The fine, easy face, the sunlight, the
dawn's talk, the plains of Tharsis *so* far below: all
conspire to please Roger. He is climbing more strong-

ly than ever, hopping up the ledges, enjoying the variety of forms exhibited by the rock. Such a beauty to rough, plated, angular, broken rock.

The face continues to lay back, and at the top of one ledge ramp they find themselves at the bottom of a giant amphitheater filled with snow. And the top of this white half-bowl is . . . sky. The top of the escarpment, apparently. Certainly nothing but sky above it. Dougal and Marie are about to start up it, and Roger joins them. Eileen stays behind to collect the others.

The technically difficult sections of the climb are done. The upper edge of the immense cliff has been rounded off by erosion, broken into alternating ridges and ravines. Here they stand at the bottom of a big bowl broken in half; at bottom the slope is about forty degrees, and it curves up to a final wall that is perhaps sixty degrees. But the bottom of the bowl is filled with deep drifts of light, dry, granular snow, sheeted with a hard layer of windslab. Crossing this stuff is difficult, and they trade the lead often. The leader crashes through the windslab and sinks to his or her knees, or even to the waist, and thereafter has to lift a foot over the windslab above, crash through again, and in that way struggle uphill through the snow. They secure the rope with deadmen—empty oxygen tanks in this case, buried deep in the snow. Roger takes his lead, and quickly begins to sweat under the glare of the sun. Each step is an effort, worse than the step before because of the increasing angle of the slope. After ten minutes he gives the lead back to Marie. Twenty minutes later it is his turn again—the other two can endure it no longer than he can. The steepness of the final wall is actually a relief, as there is less snow.

They stop to strap crampons on their boots. Starting again they fall into a slow, steady rhythm. Kick, step, kick, step; twenty of those, a stop to rest. Time goes away. They don't bother to speak when the lead changes hands: nothing to say. No one wants to break the pace. Kick, step, kick, step, kick, step. Glare of light breaking on snow. The taste of sweat.

When Roger's tenth turn in the lead comes, he sees that he is within striking distance of the top of the wall, and he resolves not to give up the lead again. The snow here is soft under windslab, and he must lean up, dig away a bit with his ice axe, swim up to the new foothold, dig away some more—on and on, gasping into the oxygen mask, sweating profusely in the suddenly overwarm clothing. . . . But he's getting closer. Dougal is behind him. He finds the pace again and sticks to it. Nothing but the pace. Twenty steps, rest. Again. Again. Again. Sweat trickles down his spine, even his feet might warm up. Sun glaring off the steep snow.

He stumbles onto flatness. It feels like some terrible error, like he might fall over the other side. But he is on the edge of a giant plateau, which swoops up in a broad conical shape, too big to be believed. He sees a flat boulder almost clear of snow and staggers over to it. Dougal is beside him, pulling oxygen mask to one side of his face: "Looks like we've topped the wall!" Dougal says, looking surprised. Gasping, Roger laughs.

As with all cliff climbs, topping out is a strange experience. After a month of vertical reality, the huge flatness seems all wrong—especially this snowy flatness that extends like a broad fan to each side. The

snow ends at the broken edge of the cliff behind them,
extends high up the gentle slope of the conical immensity before them. It is easy to believe they stand on the
flank of the biggest volcano in the solar system.

"I guess the hard part is over," Dougal says matter-
of-factly.

"Just when I was getting in shape," says Roger, and
they both laugh.

A snowy plateau, studded with black rocks, and
some big mesas. To the east, empty air: far below, the
forests of Tharsis. To the northwest, a hill sloping up
forever.

Marie arrives and dances a little jig on the boulder.
Dougal hikes back to the wall and drops into the
amphitheater again, to carry up another load. Not
much left to bring; they are almost out of food. Eileen
arrives, and Roger shakes her hand. She drops her
pack and gives him a hug. They pull some food from
the packs and eat a cold lunch while watching Hans,
Arthur, and Stephan start up the bottom of the bowl.
Dougal is already almost down to them.

When they all reach the top, in a little string led by
Dougal, the celebrating really begins. They drop their
packs, they hug, they shout, Arthur whirls in circles to
try to see it all at once, until he makes himself dizzy.
Roger cannot remember feeling exactly like this before.

"Our cache is a few kilometers south of here,"
Eileen says after consulting her maps. "If we get there
tonight we can break out the champagne."

They hike over the snow in a line, trading the lead

to break a path. It is a pleasure to walk over flat ground, and spirits are so light that they make good time. Late in the day—a full day's sunshine, their first since before Base Camp—they reach their cache, a strange camp full of tarped down, snowdrifted piles, marked by a lava causeway that ends a kilometer or so above the escarpment.

Among the new equipment is a big mushroom tent. They inflate it, and climb in through the lock and up onto the tent floor for the night's party. Suddenly they are inside a giant transparent mushroom, bouncing over the soft clear raised floor like children on a feather bed; the luxury is excessive, ludicrous, inebriating. Champagne corks pop and fly into the transparent dome of the tent roof, and in the warm air they quickly get drunk, and tell each other how marvelous the climb was, how much they enjoyed it—the discomfort, exhaustion, cold, misery, danger, and fear already dissipating in their minds, already turning into something else.

The next day Marie is not at all enthusiastic about the remainder of their climb. "It's a walk up a bloody hill! And a long walk at that!"

"How else are you going to get down?" Eileen asks acerbically. "Jump?"

It's true; the arrangements they have made force them to climb the cone of the volcano. There is a railway that descends from the north rim of the caldera to Tharsis and civilization; it uses for a rampway one of the great lava spills that erase the escarpment to the north. But first they have to get to the railway, and climbing the cone is probably the fastest, and certainly the most interesting, way to do that.

"You could climb down the cliff alone," Eileen adds sarcastically. "First solo descent. . . ."

Marie, apparently feeling the effects of last night's champagne, merely snarls and stalks off to snap herself into one of the cart harnesses. Their new collection of equipment fits into a wheeled cart, which they must pull up the slope. For convenience they are already wearing the spacesuits that they will depend on higher up; during this ascent they will climb right out of Mars's new atmosphere. They look funny in their silvery-green suits and clear helmets, Roger thinks; it reminds him of his days as a canyon guide, when such suits were necessary all over Mars. The common band of the helmet radios makes this a more social event than the cliff climb, as does the fact that all seven of them are together, four hauling the cart, three walking ahead or behind. From climb to hike: the first day is a bit anticlimactic.

On the snowy southern flank of the volcano, signs of life appear everywhere. Goraks circle them by day, on the lookout for a bit of refuse; ball owls dip around the tent at dusk like bats. On the ground Roger sees marmots on the boulders and volcanic knobs, and in the system of ravines cut into the plateau they find twisted stands of Hokkaido pine, chir pine and noctis juniper. Arthur chases a pair of Dall sheep with their curved horns, and they see prints in the snow that look like bear tracks. "Yeti," Dougal says. One mirror dusk they catch sight of a pack of snow wolves, strung out over the slope to the west. Stephan spends his spare time at the edges of the new ravines, sketching and peering through binoculars. "Come on, Roger," he says. "Let me show you those otterines I saw yesterday."

"Bunch of mutants," Roger grumbles, mostly to give Stephan a hard time. But Eileen is watching him to see his response, and dubiously he nods. What can he say? He goes with Stephan to the ravine to look for wildlife. Eileen laughs at him, eyes only, affectionately.

Onward, up the great hill. It's a six-percent grade, very regular, and smooth except for the ravines and the occasional small crater or lava knob. Below them, where the plateau breaks to become the cliff, the shield is marked by some sizeable mesas—features, Hans says, of the stress that broke off the shield. Above them, the conical shape of the huge volcano is clearly visible; the endless hill they climb slopes away to each side equally, and far away and above they see the broad, flat peak. They've got a long way to go. Wending between the ravines is easy, and the esthetic of the climb, its only point of technical interest, becomes how far they can hike every day. It's 250 kilometers from the escarpment up to the crater rim; they try for twenty-five a day, and sometimes make thirty. It feels odd to be so warm; after the intense cold of the cliff climb, the spacesuits and the mushroom tent create a distinct disconnection from the surroundings.

Hiking as a group is also odd. The common band is a continuous conversation, that one can switch on or off at will. Even when not in a mood to talk, Roger finds it entertaining to listen. Hans talks about the areology of the volcano, and he and Stephan discuss the genetic engineering that makes the wildlife around them possible. Arthur points out features that the others might take for granted. Marie complains of boredom. Eileen and Roger laugh and add a comment once in a while. Even Dougal clicks into the band around mid-afternoon, and displays a quick wit, spurring Arthur toward one amazing discovery after another. "Look at that, Arthur, it's a yeti."

"What! You're kidding! Where?"

"Over there, behind that rock."

Behind the rock is Stephan, taking a shit. "Don't come over here!"

"You liar," Arthur says.

"It must have slipped off. I think a Weddell fox was chasing it."

"You're kidding!"

"Yes."

Eileen: "Let's switch to a private band. I can't hear you over all the rest."

Roger: "Okay. Band 33."

". . . Any reason for that band in particular?"

"Ah—I think so." It *was* a long time ago, but this is the kind of weird fact his memory will pop up with. "It may be our private band from our first hike together."

She laughs. They spend the afternoon behind the others, talking.

One morning Roger wakes early, just after mirror dawn. The dull horizontal rays of the quartet of parhelia light their tent. Roger turns his head, looks past his pillow, through the tent's clear floor. Thin soil over rock, a couple of meters below. He sits up; the floor gives a little, like a gel bed. He walks over the soft plastic slowly so that he will not bounce any of the others, who are sleeping out where the cap of the roof meets the gills of the floor. The tent really does resemble a big clear mushroom; Roger descends clear steps in the side of the stalk to get to the lavatory, located down in what would be the mushroom's volvus. Emerging he finds a sleepy Eileen sponging down in the little bath next to the air compressor and regulator. "Good morning," she says. "Here, will you get my back?"

She hands him the sponge, turns around. Vigorously he rubs down the hard muscles of her back, feeling a thrill of sensual interest. That slope, where back becomes bottom: beautiful.

She looks over her shoulder. "I think I'm probably clean now."

"Ah." He grins. "Maybe so." He gives her the sponge. "I'm going for a walk before breakfast."

"Okay. Thanks."

Roger dresses, goes through the lock, walks over to the head of the meadow they are camped by: a surarctic meadow, covered with moss and lichen, and dotted with mutated edelweiss and saxifrage. A light frost coats everything in a sparkling blanket of white, and Roger feels his boots crunch as he walks.

Movement catches his eye and he stops to observe a white-furred mouse hare, dragging a loose root back to its hole. There is a flash and flutter, and a snow finch lands in the hole's entrance. The tiny hare looks up from its work, chatters at the finch, nudges past it with its load. The finch does its bird thing, head shifting instantaneously from one position to the next and then freezing in place. It follows the hare into the hole. Roger has heard of this, but he has never seen it. The hare scampers out, looking for more food. The finch appears, its head snaps from one position to the next. An instant swivel and it is staring at Roger. It flies over to the scampering hare, dive bombs it, flies off. The hare has disappeared down another hole.

Roger crosses the ice stream in the meadow, crunches up the bank. There beside a waist-high rock is an odd pure white mass, with a white sphere at the center of it. He leans over to inspect it. Slides a gloved finger over it. Some kind of ice, apparently. Unusual looking.

The sun rises and a flood of yellow light washes over the land. The yellowish white half-globe of ice at his feet looks slick. It quivers; Roger steps back. The ice is shaking free of the rock wall. The middle of the bulge cracks. A beak stabs out of the globe, breaks it open. Busy little head in there. Blue feathers, long crooked back beak, beady little black eyes. "An egg?" Roger says. But the pieces are definitely ice—he can make them melt between his gloved fingers, and feel their coldness. The bird (though its legs and breast seem to be furred, and its wings stubby, and its beak sort of fanged) staggers out of the white bubble, and shakes itself like a dog throwing off water, although it looks dry. Apparently the ice is some sort of insulation—a home for the night, or no—for the winter, no doubt. Yes. Formed of spittle or something, walling off the mouth of a shallow cave. Roger has never heard of such a thing, and he watches open-mouthed as the bird-thing takes a few running steps and glides away.

A new creature steps on the face of green Mars.

That afternoon they hike out of the realm even of the surarctic meadows. No more ground cover, no more flowers, no more small animals. Nothing now but cracks filled with struggling moss, and great mats of otoo lichen. Sometimes it is as if they walk on a thin carpet of yellow, green, red, black—splotches of color like that seen in the orbicular jasper, spread out as far as they can see in every direction, a carpet crunchy with frost in the mornings, a bit damp in the mid-day sun, a carpet crazed and parti-colored. "Amazing stuff," Hans mutters, poking at it with a finger. "Half our oxygen is being made by this wonderful symbiosis. . . ."

Late that afternoon, after they have stopped and set up the tent and tied it down to several rocks, Hans leaps through the lock waving his atmosphere kit and hopping up and down. "Listen," he says, "I just radioed the summit station for confirmation of this. There's a high pressure system over us right now. We're at 14,000 meters above the datum, but the barometric pressure is up to 350 millibars because there's a _big_ cell of air moving over the flank of the volcano this week." The others stare. Hans says, "Do you see what I mean?"

"No," exclaim three voices at once.

"High-pressure zone," Roger says unhelpfully.

"Well," Hans says, standing at attention. "It's enough to breathe! Just enough, but enough, I say. And of course no one's ever done it before—done it _this high_ before, I mean. Breathed free Martian air."

"You're kidding!"

"So we can establish the height record right here and now! I propose to do it, and I invite whoever wants to to join me."

"Now wait a minute," Eileen says.

But everyone wants to do it.

"Wait a minute," says Eileen. "I don't want everyone taking off their helmets and keeling over dead up here, for God's sake. They'll revoke my license. We have to do this in an orderly fashion. And *you*—" she points at Stephan. "You *can't* do this. I forbid it."

Stephan protests loudly and for a long time, but Eileen is adamant, and Hans agrees. "The shock could start your edema again, for sure. None of us should do it for long. But for a few minutes, it will go. Just breathe through the mesh facemasks, to warm the air."

"You can watch and save us if we keel over," Roger tells Stephan.

"Shit," Stephan says. "All right. Do it."

They gather just out from under the cap of the tent, where Stephan can, theoretically, drag them back through the lock if he has to. Hans checks his barometer one last time, nods at them. They stand in a rough circle, facing in. Everyone begins to unclip helmet latches.

Roger gets his unclipped first—the years as canyon guide have left their mark on him, in little ways like this—and he lifts the helmet up. As he places it on the ground the cold strikes his head and makes it throb. He sucks down a breath: dry ice. He refuses the urge to hyperventilate, fearful he will chill his lungs too fast and damage them. Regular breathing, he thinks, in and out. In and out. Though Dougal's mouth is covered by a mesh mask, Roger can still tell he is grinning widely. Funny how the upper face reveals that. Roger's eyes sting, his chest is frozen inside, he sucks down the frigid air and every sense quickens, breath by breath. The edges of pebbles a kilometer away are sharp and clear. Thousands of edges. "Like breathing nitrous oxide!" Arthur cries in a lilting high voice. He whoops like a little kid and the sound is odd, distant. Roger walks in a circle, on a quilt of rust lava and gaily colored patches of lichen. Intense awareness of the process of breathing seems to connect his consciousness to everything he can see; he feels like a strangely shaped lichen, struggling for air like all the rest. Jumble of rock, gleaming in the sunlight: "Let's build a cairn," he says to Dougal, and can hear his voice is wrong somehow. Slowly they step from rock to rock, picking them up and putting them in a pile. The interior of his chest is perfectly defined by each intoxicating breath. Others watching bright-eyed, sniffing, involved in their own perceptions. Roger sees his hands blur through space, sees the flesh of Dougal's face pulsing pinkly, like the flowers of moss campion. Each rock is a piece of Mars, he seems to float as he walks, the side of the volcano gets bigger, bigger, bigger; finally he is seeing it at true size. Stephan strides among them grinning through his helmet, holding up both hands. It's been ten minutes. The cairn is not yet done, but they can finish it tomorrow. "I'll make a messenger cannister for it tonight!" Dougal wheezes happily. "We can all sign it!" Stephan begins to round them all up. "Incredibly cold!" Roger says, still looking around as if he has never seen any of it before—any of anything.

Dougal and he are the last two into the lock; they shake hands. "Invigorating, eh?" Roger nods. "Very fine air."

But the air is just part of all the rest of it—part of the world, not of the planet. Right? "That's right," Roger says, staring through the tent wall down the endless slope of the mountain.

That night they celebrate with champagne again, and the party gets wild as they become sillier and sillier. Marie tries to climb the inner wall of the tent by grabbing the soft material in her hands, and falls to the floor repeatedly; Dougal juggles boots; Arthur challenges all comers to arm-wrestle, and wins so quickly they decide he is using "a trick," and disallow his victories; Roger tells government jokes ("How many ministers does it take to pour a cup of coffee?"), and institutes a long and vigorous game of spoons. He and Eileen play next to each other and in the dive for spoons they land on each other. Afterwards, sitting around the heater singing songs, she sits at his side and their legs and shoulders press together. Kid stuff, familiar and comfortable, even to those who can't remember their own childhood.

So that, that night, after everyone has gone out to the little sleeping nooks at the perimeter of the tent's circular floor, Roger's mind is full of Eileen. He remembers sponging her down that morning. Her playfulness this evening. Climbing in the storm. The long nights together in wall tents. And once again the distant past returns—his stupid, uncontrollable memory provides images from a time so far gone that it shouldn't matter any more . . . but it does. It was near the end of that trip, too. She snuck into his little cubicle and jumped him! Even though the thin panels they used to create sleeping rooms were actually much less private than what they have here; this tent is big, the air regulator is loud, the seven beds are well-spaced and divided from each other by ribbing—clear ribbing, it is true, but now the tent is dark. The cushioned floor under him (so comfortable that Marie calls it uncomfortable) gives as he moves, without even trembling a few feet away, and it never makes a sound. In short, he could crawl silently over to her bed, and join her as she once joined him, and it would be entirely discreet. Turnabout is fair play, isn't it? Even three hundred years later? There isn't much time left on this climb, and as they say, fortune favors the bold. . . .

He is about to move when suddenly Eileen is at his side, shaking his arm. In his ear she says, "I have an idea."

And afterwards, teasing: "Maybe I *do* remember you."

They trek higher still, into the zone of rock. No animals, plants, insects; no lichen; no snow. They are above it all, so high on the volcano's cone that it is getting difficult to see where their escarpment drops to the forests; two hundred kilometers away and fifteen kilometers below, the scarp's edge can only be distinguished because that's where the broad ring of snow ends. They wake up one morning and find a cloud layer a few k's downslope, obscuring the planet below. They stand on the side of an immense conical island in an even greater sea of cloud: the clouds a white wave-furrowed ocean, the volcano a great rust rock, the sky a low dark violet dome, all on a scale the mind can barely encompass. To the east, poking out of the cloud-sea, three broad peaks—an archipelago—the three Tharsis volcanoes in their well-spaced line, princes to the king Olympus. Those volcanoes, fifteen hundred kilometers away, give them a little understanding of the vastness visible. . . .

The rock up here is smoothly marbled, like a plain of petrified muscles. Individual pebbles and boulders take on an eerie presence, as if they are debris scattered by Olympian gods. Hans's progress is greatly slowed by his inspection of these rocks. One day, they find a mount that snakes up the mountain like an esker, or a Roman road; Hans explains it is a river of lava harder than the surrounding rock, which has eroded away to reveal it. They use it as an elevated road, and hike on it for all of one long day.

Roger picks up his pace, leaves the cart and the others behind. In a suit and helmet, on the lifeless face of Mars: centuries of memory flood him, he finds his breathing clotted and uneven. This is his country, he thinks. This is the transcendent landscape of his youth. It's still here. It can't be destroyed. It will always be here. He finds that he has almost forgotten, not what it looks like, but what it *feels* like to be here in such wilderness. That thought is the thorn in the exhilaration that mounts with every step. Stephan and Eileen, the other two out of harness this day, are following him up. Roger notices them and frowns. I don't want to talk about it, he thinks. I want to be alone in it.

But Stephan hikes right by him, looking over-whelmed by the desolate rock expanse, the world of rock and sky. Roger can't help but grin.

And Eileen is content just to walk with him.

Next day, however, in the harnesses of the cart, Stephan plods beside him and says, "Okay, Roger, I can see why you love this. It is sublime, truly. And in just the way we want the sublime—it's a pure land-scape, a pure place. But . . ." He plods on several more steps, and Roger and Eileen wait for him to continue, pulling in step together. "But it seems to me that you don't need the whole planet this way. This will always be here. The atmosphere will never rise this high, so you'll always have this. And the world down below, with all that life growing everywhere—it's beautiful." The beautiful and the sublime, Roger thinks. Another duality. "And maybe we need the beautiful more than the sublime?"

They haul on. Eileen looks at the mute Roger. He cannot think what to say. She smiles. "If Mars can change, so can you."

"The intense concentration of self in the middle of such a heartless immensity, my God! who can tell it?"

That night Roger seeks out Eileen, and makes love to her with a peculiar urgency; and when they are done he finds himself crying a bit, he doesn't know why; and she holds his head against her breast, until he shifts, and turns, and falls asleep.

And the following afternoon, after climbing all day up a hill that grows ever gentler, that always looks as if it will peak out just over the horizon above them, they reach flattened ground. An hour's hike, and they reach the caldera wall. They have climbed Olympus Mons.

They look down into the caldera. It is a gigantic brown plain, ringed by the round cliffs of the caldera wall. Smaller ringed cliffs inside the caldera drop to collapse craters, then terrace the round plain with round depressions, which overlap each other. The sky overhead is almost black; they can see stars, and Jupiter. Perhaps the high evening star is Earth. The thick blue rind of the atmosphere actually starts below them, so that they stand on a broad island in the middle of a round blue band, capped by a dome of black sky. Sky, caldera, ringed stone desolation. A million shades of brown, tan, red, rust, white. The planet Mars.

Along the rim a short distance stands the ruins of a Tibetan Buddhist lamasery. When Roger sees it his jaw drops. It is brown, and the main structure appears to have been a squarish boulder the size of a large house, carved and excavated until it is more air than stone. While it was occupied it must have been hermetically sealed, with airlocks in the doorways and windows fixed in place; now the windows are gone, and side buildings leaning against the main structure are broken-walled, roofless, open to the black sky. A chest-high wall of stone extends away from the out-buildings and along the rim; colored prayer wheels and prayer flags stick up from it on thin poles. Under the light touch of the stratosphere the wheels spin slowly, the flags flap limply.

* * *

"The caldera is as big as Luxembourg."
"You're kidding!"
"*No.*"

Finally even Marie is impressed. She walks to the
prayer wall, touches a prayer wheel with one hand;
looks out at the caldera, and from time to time spins
the wheel, absently.

"Invigorating view, eh?"

It will take a few days to hike around the caldera to
the railway station, so they set up camp next to the
abandoned lamasery, and the heap of brown stone is
joined by a big mushroom of clear plastic, filled with
colorful gear.

The climbers wander in the late afternoon, chatting
quietly over rocks, or the view into the shadowed
caldera. Several sections of the ringed inner cliffs look
like good climbing.

The sun is about to descend behind the rim to the
west, and great shafts of light spear the indigo sky
below them, giving the mountaintop an eerie indirect
illumination. The voices on the common band are
rapt and quiet, fading away to silence.

Roger gives Eileen a squeeze of the hand, and
wanders off by himself. The ground up here is black,
the rock cracked in a million pieces, as if the gods have
been sledge-hammering it for eons. Nothing but rock.
He clicks off the common band. It is nearly sunset.
Great lavender shafts of light spear the purple murk to
the sides, and overhead, stars shine in the blackness.
All the shadows stretch off to infinity. The bright

bronze coin of the sun grows big and oblate, slows in its descent. Roger circles the lamasery. Its western walls catch the last of the sun and cast a warm orange glaze over the ground and the ruined outbuildings. Roger kicks around the low prayer wall, replaces a fallen stone. The prayer wheels still spin—some sort of light wood, he thinks, cylinders carved with big black eyes and cursive lettering, and white paint, red paint, yellow paint, all chipped away. Roger stares into a pair of stoic Asian eyes, gives the wheel a slow spin, feels a little bit of vertigo. World everywhere. Even here. The flattened sun lands on the rim, across the caldera to the west. A faint gust of wind lofts a long banner out, ripples it slowly in dark orange air—"All right!" Roger says aloud, and gives the wheel a final hard spin and steps away, circles dizzily, tries to take in everything at once: "All right! All right. I give in. I accept."

He wipes red dust from the glass of his faceplate; recalls the little bird-thing, pecking free of clouded ice. A new creature steps on the peak of green Mars.